Jarred is in love.

Jarred drank deeply of the aromatic brew before resting the cup on the counter by the antiquated cash register. "Not much to tell," he said. "I asked Abby to come. I ran into her at the stock show and told her I needed some help decorating my new place. You know how she loves fixing things up."

"What are you talking about, your new place? You don't have a new place."

"Sure I do." Jarred grinned broadly. "Or rather, I will. Poured the foundation about a week ago. Up on Blackberry Hill."

Phillip was silent for a moment. "Let me get this straight. You saw my sister at the stock show, a little less than two weeks ago, right?"

Jarred nodded.

"You invited her to come help you decorate a house that you didn't start building until a week later?" Phillip pinned him with a reproachful look. "One that you hadn't even *mentioned* to your best friend." He lowered his cup. "You've obviously got something up your sleeve."

"Sounds pretty incriminating, doesn't it?" Jarred agreed, rubbing his jaw thoughtfully.

"Aren't you even going to deny it?"

Jarred shook his head. "Can't."

Phillip sighed in exasperation. "Then would you mind explaining it to your old buddy?"

Jarred picked up his cup and gazed into the steamy liquid. "That's easy," he said without looking up. "I'm in love with Abby."

NANCY LAVO is a gifted author from the big state of Texas where she lives with her husband and three children. Nancy is a lighthearted person who loves adding touches of comedy to her stories to balance with the more serious message of salvation.

Other books by Nancy Lavo

HEARTSONG PRESENTS
HP133—A Change of Heart
HP179—Her Father's Love

Something from Nothing

Nancy Lavo

Heartsong Presents

A note from the author:
*I love to hear from my readers! You may write to me at
the following address:*   Nancy Lavo
                          Author Relations
                          P.O. Box 719
                          Uhrichsville, OH 44683

ISBN 1-57748-247-6

SOMETHING FROM NOTHING

Cover illustration by Gary Maria.

PRINTED IN THE U.S.A.

one

"This must be just how Dorothy felt when she reached the Emerald City," Abigail Bradley murmured as she stared up at the massive double doors of the exhibition hall, "with two notable exceptions. I don't recall Dorothy complaining of a throbbing headache, nor do I remember her mentioning that her ruby slippers were too tight."

Abigail slipped off her high-heeled pump to assess the damages. It was just as she suspected. Her expensive new shoes had rubbed two angry red blisters on her heel. She heaved a discouraged sigh as she eased the shoe back over her tender foot.

None of this was part of the plan. A splitting headache and nasty blisters didn't bode well for an auspicious turning point in her life. No indeed. She'd always envisioned the big day accompanied by something nice, like—goose bumps.

The pounding in her head grew more insistent. Abigail reached into her huge handbag and located her economy size bottle of aspirin. With a practiced hand, she removed the lid, extracted the last two tablets, and popped them into her mouth. She swallowed with a grimace.

Better make a note to stop by the drugstore on the way home, she thought, tucking the empty bottle back into her bag. *Wouldn't want to face the turning point in my life without a full complement of analgesics handy.*

Her immediate needs met, it was time to face her future. Abigail's anticipation mounted as she climbed the concrete stairs. She pushed open the heavy door and stepped into the cavern-like exhibition hall now teeming with activity. People and animals moved in pleasant chaos across the dirt floor. The combined noise of man and beast echoing through the massive structure was deafening.

She paused in the entrance, the sights and sounds drawing her back to the recent past when she participated in the stock show. She could feel the excitement, the same wonderful tightness in her chest she'd experienced every year.

"Pardon me, dear."

The interruption jarred Abigail back to the present and she stepped aside to allow a corpulent woman and her prize hog to pass. She took the opportunity to flip open her notebook and study the name written at the top of the page. Bill Schraeder, Stock Show Director. She snapped the book closed and grinned. Her first assignment for the newspaper!

Her job was to locate Mr. Schraeder and pick up a list of the day's winners. It wasn't much, of course, certainly not the big society page assignment she'd been waiting for, but this was no time to split hairs. Abigail tucked the notebook under her arm and at the first opening in the crowd, plunged in to be swept along with the current.

She suffered pangs of self-consciousness as she hobbled across the barn, following the signs to the cattle building. She supposed it was her fancy blue dress and matching kid shoes that earned the curious stares from the denim-clad throng. The faux pearls at her throat probably didn't help.

The all too familiar sensation of being a square peg trying to fit in a round hole surfaced. She squelched it, raising her chin a notch and training her gaze straight ahead. It wasn't easy remaking herself. She'd pored over countless magazines to come up with what she hoped passed for sophisticated and professional. It was unfortunate she was a tad overdressed for the livestock circuit, but it couldn't be helped. The stock show was the very last place she expected to find herself today.

"I realize this is a bit unorthodox, Ms. Bradley, sending you out for the report," her boss, Mr. Robinson, had said when he called her into his office earlier that morning. "But we're a team here at the paper. And a team pulls together. With Ed out sick, you seem the logical choice for the job. After all," he continued, peering at her over his wire-rimmed glasses, "a woman from Dust Bowl is as well-suited to a stock show as any."

Abigail frowned at the memory. Dust Bowl. Why'd he bring up her hometown? She'd hoped she'd finally left it behind.

She pushed open the heavy door leading into the cattle barn and stepped inside. Things were quieter here with fewer people milling around the wooden stalls. Good. Fewer people meant she'd attract less attention.

One quick downward glance indicated she'd be too busy to notice anyway. It was obvious the cleanup crew hadn't made it to the cattle barn yet, so her full attention was needed to navigate the dung-littered floor.

She stepped carefully. Her beautiful, albeit uncomfortable, new shoes were already scuffed from her trek across the parking lot. She had no intention of totaling them in a slippery pile.

"Abby?"

A familiar deep voice rang out and she glanced up in the direction of the sound. She blinked her eyes in amazement at the attractive man advancing toward her. "Jarred?"

Having momentarily forgotten her mission to avoid disaster on the "mine-ridden" floor, she looked down just in time to see she was closing in on an enormous pile of cow manure. The combination of her high heels and momentum guaranteed she wouldn't miss it. She squeezed her eyes shut to the inevitable.

"Whoa!" Strong arms encircled her waist and lifted her high over the mountain, settling her safely on the other side. "That was a close one, honey." Jarred's dark brown eyes held a smile as he shook his head in mock exasperation. "Just like a city kid."

"Jarred!" Abigail brushed a stray lock of hair from her eyes to beam up at her friend. "What are you doing here?"

"Judging cattle." He released her slowly and stepped back. "What about you?" he asked. "What's a slick city reporter doing at the stock show? Slumming?"

She smiled wryly at his choice of words. "You could say that. Actually, the man who ordinarily covers this beat is sick and the editor asked me to fill in. Just for the day," she added hastily.

"Should'a known. Didn't figure the cattle business was society news." He flashed her a broad smile. "It's real good to see you, Abby." He shoved his hat back off his forehead as he added fondly, "It doesn't seem possible, but I believe you're prettier than ever." He lifted a strand of hair off her shoulder and rubbed it between his fingers. "Still got the goldenest hair and the bluest eyes this side of anywhere."

Abigail felt her heart slam against her ribs and her knees wobble like a newborn foal's as her eyes were drawn to his impish grin. The reaction came as no surprise. Her heart had been flip-flopping over Jarred's grin since she was twelve years old and still tagging along behind him and her big brother.

It was the dimples; she was sure of it. Jarred Worth had single-handedly devastated the entire female population of Croll County with his pearly whites and the accompanying dents in his cheeks. She suspected a part of his charm was due to the fact he was completely unaware of his appeal.

"Jarred, you old sweet-talker," she laughingly admonished him. "I gotta admit, it worries me when you're so nice. If memory serves me well, that sweet talk usually precedes some terrible practical joke you and Phillip have cooked up for me." She was suddenly serious. "How is he anyway? Do you see my brother much?"

Jarred nodded. "'Bout everyday. Your Mom and Dad, too. They're all doing fine." His gaze locked with hers. "I know they'd love to see you, Abby. It's been awhile," he scolded gently.

Abigail lowered her eyes. "I know. It's just that I'm so busy with work and all—" She stopped. All the resolutions in the world didn't make it any easier to lie to an old friend.

Jarred wrapped a comforting arm around her and squeezed gently. "It's okay, honey. I understand."

Her gaze flickered to his. Was it possible? she wondered. Did he understand? Did he know how very much she wanted to make something of herself? Could he comprehend that the price she must pay was leaving her past behind, because successes didn't come from places like Dust Bowl?

She lowered her eyes. The answer was no. He wouldn't understand, and she couldn't explain it. She'd tried once and made a terrible mess of things. She changed the subject to a safer topic. "Any idea where I can find the stock show director?"

"Sure, Bill's got an office just outside the poultry barn." He pointed toward the left. "I'd be glad to take you there."

"Thanks. He has a list of winners I'm supposed to pick up for the paper." She gave her notebook an official pat. "Guess we better get going."

Jarred placed a restraining hand on her shoulder. "You don't have to leave already, do you?"

She raised her eyes to his smiling face and for the life of her couldn't remember what her hurry was about. "Well, uh—"

He rubbed his jaw thoughtfully. "I've got to judge Herefords at eight, then I'm through for the evening." His eyes lit up. "Could you come back then? We could catch up on old times." He hit her with another dazzling grin. "What do you say?"

His smile had gained potency over the past year, she noted wryly. Breathless and addled, she nodded her assent without thinking. Who was she to refuse those glorious dimples?

Even as she agreed, a niggling doubt troubled her—something about tonight. A date!

"Oh, wait! I can't make it tonight. I've got other plans tonight. A date."

"No problem," Jarred said as he took her arm and skillfully directed her through the manure-minefield toward the director's office. "Bring him along."

Abigail nearly laughed as she struggled to keep up with him, limping along by his side. Edward Winters going to the stock show? "I don't think so—"

Jarred dismissed her argument with a wave of his hand. "Here's Bill's office," he said, motioning toward an open door. "I'll run along and let you two get down to business."

She opened her mouth to protest. "Jarred, about tonight—"

Before she could finish, he stunned her into silence by planting a kiss on her forehead and walking away. "See you at eight, Abby," he called over his shoulder as he headed toward the cattle barn. "Barn Three."

Abigail watched his retreat in astonishment. "He kissed me. Jarred Worth kissed me," she whispered as her fingertips absently traced the place where his lips touched her. She sighed. "I suppose it wouldn't hurt to stop by for just a few minutes."

"Ahem, can I help you?"

Abigail whipped her head around in surprise. She hadn't heard the man come up behind her. "Oh! Yes, I'm Abigail Bradley," she said, silently congratulating herself on her quick recovery. She extended her hand to shake his. "I'm from the—" She stopped to stare in amazement at her outstretched arm.

It was covered with goose bumps.

two

"Now tell me again, Abigail, why it is we are going to the stock show," Edward's expression was pained, "instead of the club like we had planned?"

Good question, Abigail thought dismally. *Why am I dragging Oklahoma's most prominent citizen to a barn, when he invited me to his country club, the most exclusive club in the city?*

Actually, she knew the answer. Jarred's dimples.

She lifted her most beguiling smile to the handsome man walking beside her. "Didn't I explain? I'm so sorry." Abigail hoped her voice sounded cultured. "You see, I was at the stock show this morning, on newspaper business, and I ran into an old family friend. When he asked us to drop by for a minute, to catch up on old times, I couldn't refuse." She sighed dramatically. "Family obligations can be so touchy." She placed a freshly manicured hand on Edward's bronzed arm. "You've been so accommodating and I want you to know how very much I appreciate you doing this for me."

He favored her with an understanding smile. "I'm glad to do it. No sense in offending family friends." He wrinkled his aristocratic nose. "I wish we could find a place that smells better."

"Smells better?" Abigail sniffed. She hadn't noticed the pungent smell of livestock and hay until he mentioned it. The familiar barnyard aroma had been a big part of her life for so long that it was no longer noteworthy. But, she reminded herself, that was the old Abigail. The one she was leaving behind. "Oh yes, the smell." She fanned her face delicately. "Appalling."

Edward and Abigail arrived in Barn Three to find the judging already in progress. The lower half of the metal bleachers was filled, forcing them to climb through the crowd to find a seat at the top.

"I can't believe that of all these people," Edward grumbled when they reached a vacant seat, "not a one of them can think of something better to do than to watch cows."

"Shhh," Abigail smiled sweetly while placing a slender finger against her lips. "Someone will hear you."

She remained standing to scan the arena floor. "Oh look," she whispered, pointing toward the center of the room. "There's Jarred. He's the one in the red shirt."

"What's he doing out there?"

"He's a judge." Abigail took her seat next to Edward. "See his clipboard? He's rating the cattle in different categories to determine the Grand Champion."

Edward turned to study her. "Are you trying to tell me he can actually tell the difference between one cow and the next?"

"Absolutely!" Abigail's voice grew more animated. "Take number seven, for example. She's a winner for sure." She nodded confidently as she looked over at the animal. "Why just look at her back; see how flat it is? And her legs, notice how long they are—"

She stopped in mid-sentence. What was she doing? Only a hayseed would know the particulars of cattle judging. And the new Abigail Bradley was no hayseed.

She shrugged, trying to appear indifferent. "What I mean is, I guess he can tell. After all, he's a cattle breeder." She tossed him a weak smile before settling back against the bleachers.

Her head began to ache, which came as no surprise considering the way her evening was going. Her very important date was quickly turning out very wrong. She'd supplied Edward with a convincing display of her lack of sophistication and he was no doubt disgusted with her. Not that she could blame him.

As discreetly as possible she slipped her hand into the back pocket of her jeans and pulled out the flat travel pack of aspirin she carried. She popped open the lid, tipped two round tablets into the palm of her hand, and gulped them down.

She stole a covert glance at her date, who seemed to have developed an interest in the proceedings on the arena floor. She relaxed a bit. Maybe the evening could be salvaged after all. They'd spend a few minutes reminiscing with Jarred and there would still be plenty of time to go to the club. Piece of cake.

She was smiling with renewed self-confidence when her attention drifted down to the arena floor where Jarred had narrowed the field of competitors to three. An expectant hush settled over the capacity crowd as he made his final appraisal of the animals.

Abigail leaned forward on the bleacher, her lower lip caught between her teeth. She could see the tension on Jarred's face as he studied the contenders. This would be a tough call. Any one of the three cows was prize-worthy, but only one would earn the title of Grand Champion.

Her heart raced as Jarred lowered his clipboard. The decision was made. The instant he walked over to number seven and slapped the cow on the rump, indicating his selection as Grand Champion, Abigail was on her feet.

"I knew it!" she shouted, jumping up and down and clapping wildly. She was about to tuck two fingers into her mouth and let out a whistle of appreciation when she happened to catch a glimpse of Edward from the corner of her eye.

He was still seated, his handsome jaw sagging as he studied her with a wide-eyed stare. He was clearly shocked.

Perhaps she should explain.

"You know, Edward," she began as she lowered herself demurely to the bleacher and folded her hands in her lap. "My parents have always placed special emphasis on the importance of a well-rounded education." *That would certainly be news to them,* her conscience accused. Abigail ignored it and went on, "When I was twelve, I had the opportunity to participate in a livestock exhibition similar to this one—"

Edward's expression remained unchanged. He stared at her as though she'd sprouted horns.

"Uh, well, yes, uh never mind," she stammered, scrambling to her feet. "Let's go find Jarred."

Jarred caught sight of them descending the bleachers and waited at the bottom. "Abby!" He wrapped her in a bear hug.

Abigail stiffened at the sound of her inelegant nickname. She separated herself from Jarred's embrace, straightened her shoulders, and lifted her chin. "It's Abigail, Jarred. I go by Abigail now."

"Ahhh." Jarred nodded sagely, his brown eyes dancing with mirth. "Abigail." He extended a hand toward Edward. "Hi, you must be Abigail's date. I'm Jarred Worth."

Edward seemed to size him up before accepting his hand. "Edward Winters. Interesting program tonight."

Jarred flashed him a smile. "Glad you enjoyed it. Did Abby, uh I mean Abigail, tell you about her experiences in the ring? She had the prettiest little heifer—" He turned to Abigail. "What was her name?"

Abigail glared a warning at Jarred. "I don't think Edward wants to hear about cows right now, Jarred." She favored Edward with a sweet smile. "In fact, we've got to run. He and I are on our way to the club."

"Nonsense," Edward declared. "You two haven't had an opportunity to visit yet. May I suggest the three of us go someplace quiet where we can really talk?" He turned to Abigail. "Is the offer for coffee at your place still open?"

"My place?" Abigail squeaked.

"Sure. I'd love to see it and I'll bet Jarred would too." He looked to Jarred who nodded his confirmation. "Furthermore, it would be quiet enough for you two to catch up on family news."

Abigail was certain her mouth hung open like a fish as she heard her plans disintegrate. "You're sure you don't want to go to the club?" she asked.

Edward shook his head. "There's plenty of time for the club another day. What do you say, Jarred. Can you make it?"

Jarred grinned. "Sounds great."

❧

What a contrast, Abigail mused as she studied the two men engaged in a lively conversation around the coffee table in her living room. They were approximately the same age and height, with Jarred maybe an inch or two taller, but the similarities ended there.

Jarred sat on her right, one long muscular leg folded across the other, his boot-clad ankle resting on his knee. His big frame dwarfed the over-stuffed chair he occupied. There was a rough look about him, a rugged outdoorsy sort of look, completely incompatible with the delicately patterned chintz chair. He was a man better suited to leather, she decided.

Edward, however, looked right at home beside her on the brocade couch, his slender arm draped behind her. He was obviously a man to whom luxury was second nature.

Jarred laughed, a deep warm laugh, and Abigail's eyes were

drawn back to him. He was attractive in an unrefined, wholesome way. He didn't have Edward's polish and drop-dead good looks, but she suspected Jarred was the type who always looked terrific, even first thing in the morning. She tried not to think about his dimples.

She watched as Jarred raked a hand through his hair that fell in thick dark waves over the top of his collar. He'd always said he wore it long in self-defense. Any shorter and it curled up into annoying ringlets. Abigail smiled in approval. It wasn't stylish, but it was absolutely right for him.

She peeked at her date for comparison. He wore his tawny hair cropped short and molded into the latest European style with a liberal application of mousse. Very chic.

Jarred's clothes, jeans and a red twill shirt, were the clothes of a working man—clean, comfortable, and utilitarian. Edward wore his cleaner-creased designer jeans and polo shirt with the well-bred elegance of a man to whom working with his hands meant flipping the pages of a stock report.

A man of the earth. A man of the world.

What a contrast.

Jarred glanced at his watch. "Look at the time! Guess I'd better be running along. Judging starts first thing in the morning." He set his glass of iced tea on the coffee table and rose to his feet. "I've got to hand it to you," he said, chucking Abigail affectionately under the chin. "This is a showplace. I never realized you were such a talented decorator." He gestured around the room. "Your apartment looks like something out of a magazine."

She dropped her gaze. "That's sweet of you to say, but really, it's nothing."

Edward stood to join him. "She's being too modest. I've been in this apartment complex before. Plain vanilla." He rested a hand on her shoulder. "Abigail's got a real gift for making something from nothing."

The three of them walked toward the front door. "I've enjoyed the evening," Jarred said with genuine warmth. He shook Edward's hand. "Pleasure meeting you, Edward. And Abby," he corrected himself with an unrepentant grin, "I mean Abigail, I'll be sure to tell your parents hello for you."

He tipped his hat before swinging open the front door and stepping outside. "Good night."

Edward and Abigail watched in silence as Jarred climbed into his truck and drove away.

"I guess I'll be running along, too." Edward's voice interrupted the stillness of the evening. "I know you've got to be at work early in the morning."

Abigail blinked back her disappointment. Although Edward had been a good sport and even appeared to enjoy the evening, she knew he was disillusioned with her. She had known all along she was no match for his high-born sophistication, but now he must realize it too. She *was* a square peg trying to fit into a round hole. What made her think she could ever fit in?

"Edward, I've had a lovely evening." She lowered her gaze to her tightly clasped hands. "I'm sorry things worked out so differently from what we had planned. You've been very kind humoring me about the stock show."

"Not at all," Edward said with a magnanimous wave of his hand. "I had a marvelous time." He must have seen the look of disbelief on her face because he added, "I mean it. I found the evening fascinating, and I must say I owe that to you."

"To me?"

Edward nodded. "Absolutely. It was something you said at the stock show. You told me that your parents insisted upon you receiving a well-rounded education, and that livestock exhibitions were included."

"Yes, well—" Abigail began guiltily.

"It was then," he interrupted, "I realized the shortcomings in my own education. I've had no experience with that sort of thing, until now." He took her hands in his. "Do you know, in my twenty-eight years, I'd never met a real cowboy. Until tonight."

"Jarred's a rancher," Abigail corrected softly.

Edward appeared not to hear. "I must say, I'm glad I followed my instincts about bringing him here instead of inviting him to the club."

Was that condescension she heard in his voice? "I'm sorry?"

"Please don't misunderstand me. I thought your friend was a decent enough guy, but let's face it, a cowboy—"

"Jarred's a rancher."

"Yes, thank you, a rancher," he conceded, "would be completely out of his element at a country club. More at home in a barn." He raised a refined brow. "I couldn't help but notice he smelled of—well, you know, cow leavings. I imagine his sort of people, barn types, all do."

Abigail studied her hands self-consciously. Being a reformed "barn type," she sincerely hoped he was wrong. The worst part was, she had smelled it too. The distinct aroma of cow manure.

Edward lifted her chin with his forefinger. "We're kindred spirits, you and I," he said softly.

Abigail couldn't believe her ears. "We are?"

He chuckled. "I love your sense of humor, Abigail. I'd like to call you again."

"You would? Uh, I mean, I'd like that."

He bent to kiss her. "Good night then."

"Good night."

She watched his retreating figure, the warm glow of victory suffusing through her. She'd been worried sick that she'd ruined her important date and instead he thought they were two of a kind. She smiled smugly at the thought. *Cultured. Refined. Sophisticated.*

It was then she happened to glance down at Edward's right shoe. The lights along the sidewalk showed the entire heel of his loafer was caked in—no, it couldn't be. She squinted to be sure.

It was true.

The entire heel of his expensive, imported loafer was caked in cow manure.

three

All five feet, ten inches, one hundred twenty-two pounds of Lurline Pettigrew was poised and ready to pounce on Abigail when she arrived at her cubicle the following morning.

"Well," she demanded. "How was it?"

"How was what?" Abigail asked with exaggerated innocence.

Lurline rolled her eyes. "Your date with destiny, of course!"

Abigail repressed a grin as she took her time sitting down on her chair, tucking her purse away in the bottom drawer of her scarred metal file cabinet, and arranging the stacks of paper on her desk. She finally took pity on her friend who looked as though she might explode. "It was fabulous," she admitted with a dreamy sigh. "Even better than I imagined."

"I knew it!" Lurline pulled a chair up beside Abigail's. "Go on," she coaxed. "Tell me. I want to hear every last detail."

Abigail laughed. "It all started when we went to the stock show."

"The stock show!" Lurline screeched. She glanced sheepishly around the room before lowering her voice, "I thought you were going to his club."

"Yes, well, that was before I met Jarred and he asked me to stop by the stock show."

"Jarred?" Lurline was obviously bewildered. "Who's Jarred?"

"An old family friend."

"You're telling me," Lurline's voice rose dangerously once again, "you wasted a perfect evening with the man *Oklahoma Magazine* voted 'most eligible bachelor' to spend it with an old family friend?"

"Sounds crazy, I know," Abigail acknowledged. "But trust me, I had no choice. It was the dimples."

"Dimples? None of the magazine articles I've read about Edward ever mentioned dimples."

"Not Edward, silly. Jarred."

Lurline wrinkled her freckled nose. "I'm confused."

"Don't be. It's really very simple. Edward and I had a lovely time. In fact, he asked if he could call me again."

"Yes!" Lurline clasped her hands over her heart and squealed. "This is big! This is really big! I read an article in the *Tribune* that quoted Edward as saying he made it a point to never date the same woman twice."

"Oh." Abigail's face fell. "Maybe he just said it to be nice."

"Are you kidding? Gorgeous millionaire bachelors don't have to be nice. He must have really liked you." She took Abigail squarely by the shoulders and fixed her with an earnest gaze. "It's happening, just like you said. You're gonna make something of yourself, Abigail. You're gonna be somebody important. You know, with highfalutin friends and connections at the top. A real success. I can just feel it."

Abigail closed her eyes for a moment to savor the idea. Abigail Bradley—the success. Was it finally going to happen?

Actually, up until recently, she'd been operating under the misconception that she was already a success. Growing up in Dust Bowl, she believed having a warm, loving family, supportive friends, and her faith in the Almighty meant fulfillment. The thought brought a wry smile to her face. How naive she had been. Her thoughts drifted back to her early days at college, to the first time she realized those simple things weren't enough.

Abigail had not taken college lightly. To her, college attendance was a privilege. And with the privilege came responsibility. Her family scrimped and saved for years to put aside enough money to send her to school. She resolved to make the most of her four years, to learn everything she could to ensure her family's sacrifice was not in vain.

She'd been on the campus less than twenty-four hours when she had her first, most unforgettable lesson.

She'd spent the better part of two hours standing in line for an interview with Dean Henderson, the dean of freshman. Over the course of the meeting, the two of them were to decide on her major. Abigail was a bundle of nerves by the time she knocked on the glass pane of the office door of such an exalted personage.

"Come in."

Abigail entered and took the seat across the desk as the man indicated.

"You're Abigail Bradley?" he asked without looking up.

"Yes, sir."

He leaned back in his chair and folded his arms across his chest. "Before we discuss possible majors, I'd like to learn a little bit about you. Tell me, Ms. Bradley, what are your plans for the future? Where do you see yourself ten years from now?"

Abigail pursed her lips as she tried to conjure up a picture of the future. A sudden smile lit her face. "If all goes well, I see myself as a wife and mother."

He waited a full thirty seconds before unfolding his arms and leaning across the desk to squint at her through horn-rimmed glasses. "Is that all?"

"I'm sorry?"

"Being a wife and mother is the sum total of your aspirations? You have no plans to use your talents? To make something of yourself?"

Abigail was struck dumb. "Well no," she said finally, "I mean yes. I thought that would be making something of myself."

"You're from—" Dean Henderson glanced down at her file. "Dust Bowl, I see. That explains a great deal."

"Does it?"

"Absolutely." He leaned across the desk to confide, "I was a country boy myself. Born and raised in Rock Junction."

Abigail relaxed a fraction. "Really?"

"My years in Rock Junction were some of the happiest I've known, but as much as I enjoyed them, I fear the experiences there left me wholly unprepared for life."

He laid her file on the desk and regarded her solemnly. "Your response to my question about your plans for the future indicates to me you are laboring under the same false information I was. In fact, many of my rural students come to the University with similar aspirations. They attend school, and even earn a degree, but rather than going on to make something of themselves, they want to go home, take any job, marry, and raise a family, just as their parents did, depending on their religion and relationships to make their lives count for something."

Abigail swallowed hard at the succinct summation. That was her life in a nutshell.

"The problem is," Dean Henderson continued, "the simplistic

thinking that says God and family should be the epicenter of life sounds good, but it has no basis in reality. Maybe it was true once, for our parents' generation or their parents, but not anymore. It's no longer enough. Educated people need more. Out here in the real world, you can't make God and family the focus of your life—you'd stagnate in unfulfillment."

"But—"

He raised his hand to silence her objection. "You are young, Ms. Bradley and haven't seen much of the world. Take the word of a man who has; you've got to make something of yourself. You will find, as I did, that a person's identity—his value to himself and society—is tied to what he accomplishes. Achievement, wealth, power, success—these are the things that make life worth living. Settle for anything less and you'll be miserable."

A heaviness settled in the pit of her stomach. "I had no idea."

"Don't feel badly, Ms. Bradley." He leaned forward and rested his elbows on the desk. "I see many students each year who start out thinking as you do. They are often able to go beyond their rural roots and achieve a measure of success."

He flipped open her file again. "I see you've chosen English as a major, and rightly so considering your strength in that subject. I wonder, though, if I might make a suggestion."

"Certainly."

"I'd like to see you pursue journalism as a major, instead of English. It would require the strong English skills you possess, and upon graduation it would place you in a wide open field with plenty of room for finding success. Of course, making something of yourself is totally up to you."

Taking her weak nod as assent, Dean Henderson made a notation in her file and closed the folder. "That takes care of our business for today. It was a pleasure meeting you, Ms. Bradley. With our backgrounds, I feel we have much in common."

The interview concluded, Abigail rose to her feet. "Do you get back to Rock Junction much?"

"No. Not for many years. The people there couldn't understand what I was trying to do with my life, and I found their well-meaning advice stifling."

Dean Henderson stood and walked around the desk to stand

at the door with Abigail. "There was nothing back there for me. The wisest course of action for me was to make a clean break from the past."

Abigail had walked out of the interview that day a different person. For the very first time she doubted the direction she'd had all her life.

&

"Well, well, what do we have here?"

Abigail's head snapped up, her colorful dream fading to black. "Hello, Suzanne." Her voice was decidedly cool as she greeted the willowy blond. "What brings you down here?"

"She just slithered in to spread a little sunshine," Lurline muttered.

"Oh! Lurline, is that you? I hardly recognized you under that home perm." Suzanne circled her in critical appraisal. "Tsk tsk. You really ought to consider going to a professional."

"Why don't you just crawl back under your rock?"

Abigail raised a hand to silence her friend. "Was there something you needed, Suzanne?" she asked tightly.

"No need to sound so testy. I just dropped by to see how your assignment at the stock show went."

"What are you talking about?"

"Don't be coy with me, Abigail. I know Robinson sent you to pick up the judging results." Suzanne smirked. "After all, it was my idea."

Abigail's brows shot up. "I beg your pardon?"

"She's just talking," Lurline said. She lowered her voice to a stage whisper. "Ignore her. Maybe she'll go away."

Suzanne was not deterred. "It's true," she said, bobbing her bleached blond head emphatically. "When the need for someone to cover the stock show came up at the staff meeting, I suggested Abigail." She picked a piece of nonexistent lint from the sleeve of her expensive silk suit. "I know you're an aspiring reporter, Abigail, and I wanted to help you. I felt something of this nature could showcase your talents—considering your background, I mean. Evidently the others weren't aware you're a Dust Bowl girl."

Lurline bristled. "Something wrong with Dust Bowl?"

"Not at all. I'm sure it's a charming place," Suzanne's voice dripped with saccharin.

"Who knows, Abigail," Suzanne persisted, "if things continue on like this, one day you might have your own byline. I can see it now," she said, framing an imaginary headline in the air with her perfectly manicured fingers. "ABIGAIL BRADLEY—TALES FROM THE BARNYARD." She glimpsed the diamond encrusted watch on her wrist. "Oh, look at the time. Sorry I can't stay and chat, girls. I've got a story to finish." She strode to the hallway before calling out, "The work of a reporter is never done."

"That's it!" Lurline growled as she jumped from her chair. She pushed up her shirt sleeves, exposing bony forearms. "I'm going to punch her out!"

Abigail stood up and placed her hands on her loyal friend's slender shoulders, gently pushing her back into her seat. "It's not worth it, Lurline."

Lurline sank back into her chair. "I guess you're right," she admitted glumly. "Although, I don't know how you can be so casual about it. Suzanne's done nothing but needle you ever since she got her daddy to get her your society page job."

"We can't be sure," Abigail protested weakly.

"Oh yes we can." Lurline was emphatic. "Everybody knows Robinson thinks you're the better writer." She leaned toward Abigail to whisper, "Scuttlebutt is he went to bat for you—took it all the way to the top, but Daddy Megabucks, majority stock-holder of the paper, had final say, and he wanted his little Suzanne to get the job." She clenched and unclenched her fists. "The whole idea makes me sick."

Abigail knew just how she felt. It made her sick too. The memory was still vivid enough to make her stomach queasy and her temples throb. She slid open her top drawer and rummaged through the contents, finally retrieving the bonus size bottle of aspirin. She washed down two tablets with the dregs from her coffee cup.

"It hasn't been all bad." Abigail grinned into the sympathetic face of her friend. "After all, if I had gotten the society page job, I might never have met you."

Lurline slapped her on the back. "And we have a pretty fine

time down here in the catacombs, don't we?" She stood up. "Guess me and my bad perm will be shoving off. It's a mighty big responsibility to shoulder when people are *dying* for you to write about them."

Abigail groaned. "I'm not sure I'll ever get used to obituary humor. And Lurline," she added, with a quick glance at the pile of springy orange curls on top of her friend's head, "I like your hair. I don't think it looks bad at all."

"Thanks, pal. I appreciate the vote of confidence, even if you are a lousy liar." Lurline walked a few steps away, paused, and hurried back to drop into the chair beside Abigail once more. "Hey, I almost forgot to ask." She lowered her voice to a whisper. "Did he kiss you?"

"Hmmm?" Abigail's attention was directed to the stack of mail on her desk.

"Edward, silly. Did he kiss you?"

Abigail raised her eyes to Lurline's. "Yes."

"That's all you have to say about it?" Her disappointment was clear. "Just yes?"

Abigail shrugged apologetically.

"Abigail, this is me, your old buddy Lurline. You can tell me. Was it great? You know, did you feel kinda weak-kneed? See fireworks? Hear wedding bells?"

Abigail tried to remember the kiss in detail, and found she could not. She shook her head. "No, not that I remember. Of course, it was just a little kiss."

Lurline sprang to her feet, her hands resting on her hips. "Girl," she huffed, "when we're talking about Edward Winters, Mr. Right, the top rung of Oklahoma society—ain't no such thing as a little kiss." With that she turned and walked slowly down the hall, shaking her head as she went. Abigail could hear her muttering, "Couldn't even remember the kiss. I would have expected a good case of goose bumps, at the very least."

four

Herbal savvy seminar. Meet author Agnes Fescue. She'll discuss herbs that keep us healthy and energi. . .

The shrill ring of the telephone stopped Abigail in midkeystroke. She grabbed the receiver, anchoring it under her chin. "Bradley, Notebook."

"Hey, Abigail," chirped a familiar voice. "I just sent a visitor down your way."

"Aw Lurline, not now," she wailed. "It's four-thirty and I've still got three columns of entries before deadline."

"Sorry, girl. I knew you'd be busy, but I just couldn't say no." She giggled before adding, "Must have been the dimples."

"Dimples? Did you say dimples?" Abigail demanded of the receiver. "Lurline?"

Click.

Abigail stared at the now dead phone. "Dimples?"

The painful beginnings of a headache took priority over Lurline's cryptic message. She began rifling through the contents of her desk drawer for her aspirin. Her arms were buried up to her elbows in clutter, searching for the elusive plastic bottle when a cheerful voice called out from behind her. "Hi, honey! Got a minute?"

Jarred! The sound of his deep voice blanketed her with a comforting warmth, much like a well-worn quilt on a cold evening. Yet, at the same time, it seemed to spark every nerve in her body to life.

She swung her chair around quickly. "Jarred? What a surprise!"

As he pulled his hat from his head, he hit her with a full blown smile, exposing perfect white teeth and making his dimples more pronounced. Her heart threw itself against her ribs, and she was heartily thankful for the solid support of the chair beneath her.

"I hope you don't mind me dropping by like this," he said, dragging out the chair beside hers and straddling it like he would a horse. "I was on my way out of town when I had this brainstorm and I was wondering if you could do me a favor."

Looking up into the face of her lifelong friend, she knew she was helpless. If he asked her to jump off the building she'd be powerless to refuse. Maybe if she couldn't see his dimples she'd have a fair chance.

She averted her gaze to her clasped hands resting in her lap. "I'll be glad to help you if I can, Jarred," she said, focusing determinedly on a chip in the polish on her thumbnail. "What is it you need?"

"A little of your expertise."

He grinned when she glanced up with a puzzled expression, and continued, "I finally got around to building out on my property."

"A house? I didn't know that."

Jarred slanted her a wry look. "You haven't been home to see."

"True," she admitted sheepishly. "I'm sorry, Jarred, I don't follow—"

"Simple. I need a decorator. You know, someone to help me pull it all together. Living in Dust Bowl has severely limited my selection."

Abigail laughed. "I'll say. Is there even one decorator there?"

Jarred shook his head. "Not a one. Unless you count Irma Griggs."

"Irma? What are her credentials?"

"All of her plastic ware is color coordinated, and she keeps a regular subscription to the mail order catalog. By Dust Bowl standards, she's a decorating whiz."

Abigail giggled.

"Anyway, I thought maybe you'd consider helping me out. I saw your place. It's beautiful. Real homey. According to your friend, Edward, you made something from nothing." His gaze locked with hers. "I'd like you to help me do that with mine."

"Oh, I don't know, Jarred," she shook her head slowly.

His disappointment was clear. "Think it might cause a problem with your fella?"

"My fella?"

"Yeah, you know, ol' Edward what's-his-name."

Abigail smiled. "He's not my fella, Jarred. I hardly know him. We only went out that one time."

Jarred's wide grin was back in place. "Good, then I don't see a problem. Can you come home, say, next weekend and we can get started?"

"Really, I'd like to, Jarred, but—" She lowered her eyes to avoid his steady gaze. How could she explain? She couldn't go back to Dust Bowl, not after all the things she said. Even if she hadn't said all those things, Dust Bowl wasn't in her plans. Not even for Jarred.

He reached over, capturing her small hands in his large ones. "I'm asking too much of our friendship, aren't I?" he asked, as his dark eyes searched her face. "Look, I should've known you were too busy, what with all you do here at the paper. I'm sorry for putting you on the spot."

Abigail risked lifting her eyes to his for just a second. She was broadsided by his tender smile. "I'm glad I got a chance to see you one last time before I went home." He squeezed her hand gently and started to get up.

"Wait! Don't go. I'll do it."

Jarred lowered himself back onto the chair. His expression was hopeful. "Are you sure?"

She nodded, never being any less sure of anything in her life. *Return to Dust Bowl? I must be nuts.* "I'll come. But I'd like to try and get all the work done next weekend. I don't want to have to come back."

She could see he was stung by her words and she tried to soften them with a little white lie. "It's just that I'm buried in paperwork here." She pointed toward the stack of papers on her desk. "I don't feel like I could spend any more time away."

Jarred nodded. "I understand, honey."

He got to his feet. "Don't let me keep you. I can see you have plenty to do." He bent and dropped a quick kiss on her brow before turning to leave. "See you next weekend, Abby." He paused in the doorway to add softly, "And thanks."

"You're welcome," she whispered, watching his tall form disappear into the hall.

Lurline appeared several minutes later to find Abigail staring at the empty doorway. "What'cha looking at?"

The question startled her. "Me?" Abigail gave her head a quick shake. "Nothing."

Lurline continued to study her. "You cold, Abigail?"

"No." Abigail quirked a brow. "Why do you ask?"

Lurline pointed to Abigail's crossed arms. "'Cuz your arms are covered in goose bumps."

❧

It was late, after eight o'clock, when Abigail pulled her dinner out of the microwave and placed it on the table in her small kitchen. It smelled delicious. Lasagna was always one of her favorites. She poured herself a glass of water from the plastic pitcher she kept in the refrigerator and sat down to eat.

Abigail bowed her head in prayer, a holdover from her childhood. Her family never ate before giving thanks. The blessing over her meals was one of the few times she spoke to God anymore. "Dear God, bless this food. Amen."

She took a bite, chewing thoughtfully. Her mind had been racing since her meeting with Jarred that afternoon. *Why on earth did I agree to go back to Dust Bowl?* she wondered, stabbing a noodle with her fork. Hadn't she vowed never to return?

She grimaced at the torturous memory.

Two days after her graduation from college, with a master's degree in journalism, Abigail interviewed for a job at the city newspaper. The Friday morning interview with David Robinson, editor of the *Herald,* went smoothly.

"I like your work, Ms. Bradley," he had said, after leafing through her portfolio. "You've got real style. We can use you here at the *Herald*."

Abigail leaned forward so quickly she nearly fell out of her seat. "Does that mean you have a position open?"

Mr. Robinson laughed at her unbridled enthusiasm. "Several. I've got to get the approval of management, of course, but my recommendation would be to place you in the Society Department."

"The Society Department?" Abigail gasped. The thought was almost too good to be true. She'd be a high-powered reporter for the *Herald*. And that would make her a success in anybody's book. "When do I start?"

Robinson threw up his hands. "Not so fast, Ms. Bradley. I've got to get you approved first." He glanced down at the calendar on his desk. "We meet at four o'clock this afternoon." He lifted his eyes to meet hers. "I should know something by Monday morning. Can you come in, say nine o'clock Monday morning, and we'll talk?"

"You bet I can!" She stood up and collected her portfolio from the desk. "Thanks, Mr. Robinson," she said, pumping his hand enthusiastically. "It was a pleasure talking with you. I look forward to seeing you on Monday."

Abigail had restrained herself long enough to get out of the building before she let out a shrill whistle of delight. "Yippee! Look out world, here I come!" She climbed into her new red car, a luxury purchased with part of the small inheritance she received from her grandmother, and raced the one hundred fifty miles home to share the news with her parents.

"Mom! Dad!" she shouted, as she burst through the front door. "I got it! I got the job!"

Her mother appeared from the kitchen, dusting off her floured palms on the worn apron tied around her ample waist. "What job are you talking about, Abby?"

"Reporter," she said breathlessly, "for the *Herald*."

"The *Herald*? You don't mean the big city paper downtown?"

Abigail nodded. "That's the one." She thumped her chest with her thumb. "You're looking at the new society page reporter for the *Herald*."

Her mother didn't appear to share her enthusiasm.

"But, honey," she began, wrapping her arm around her daughter's waist, "you'd be so far from home. Wouldn't you rather talk to that nice Mr. Stuck down at the *Dust Bowl Digest*? I bet he'd be delighted to give you a job.

"Why sure," her mother continued, "you can work for him and still live at home. We'll fix up your room. You've always talked about painting it. Maybe a nice shade of pink. And some new curtains. Yes, we'll get some pretty new curtains from the mail order catalog."

Abigail couldn't believe her ears. She'd landed the job of a lifetime and her mother wanted to talk about curtains. "No, Mom, you don't understand. I don't want to move back!" She immediately regretted her bluntness as she watched tears pool in her mother's dark eyes.

"It's not that I wouldn't like to, exactly," she explained more gently, silently willing her mother to understand just how important this job was. "It's just that this is an opportunity for me to be a success. To use my college education. To make something of myself."

Two fat tears slid down her mother's cheek. Obviously, she didn't understand.

The meeting with her father went no better. "How's my little girl?" he asked, popping his head inside her bedroom door when he arrived home for dinner. "Momma says you've got troubles."

Abigail sighed heavily. "Not troubles, Daddy. Opportunity. I've got a job with the *Herald*. Society page reporter."

Her father walked in and sat on the bed beside her, shaking his gray head. "That comes as a mighty big surprise from a girl who's always talked of settling down in Dust Bowl. You've been planning on buying the Nugent place and raising a big family for as long as I can remember. Now if it's work you're after, you don't need to go all the way to the big city to get a job. Heavens, I've got an idea old Mr. Stuck at the *Digest* would be proud to have you work for him. He runs a first class paper. Did Momma tell you it's coming out twice weekly now?"

He scratched his whiskered chin for a moment. "'Course, I don't know if he has any openings for a society reporter. Fact is, I'm not at all certain Dust Bowl has any society, but I'm sure you two could work something out."

Abigail wanted to laugh out of sheer frustration. A society page in Dust Bowl? *Sure, and pigs fly.* "Daddy, I don't want to work for the *Digest!* I want to work for the *Herald!* I've got to get out of Dust Bowl and make something of myself. I want to find fulfillment. I want to be a success!"

Father and daughter regarded one another in uncomfortable silence.

Finally, it was her father that broke it. "Honey," he said gently, taking her small smooth hands in his large callused ones, "I can understand your need to try out your wings. I was young once myself."

"I know, Daddy." It was hard to stay mad at him when he grinned at her like that.

"It's just that I had to learn so many things the hard way, darlin', and I don't want you to have to do the same. You don't have to go far away to some big fancy job to be fulfilled. Truth is, it ain't what you do, or how much you make, or even who you're married to that makes you a success. It's Whose you are."

Abigail studied her beloved father as he spoke. She knew he was a wise man. His was not the book-learned wisdom of an intellectual, but a simple wisdom acquired through living, and grounded in his deep faith in God. As a child she'd accepted his counsel without reservation.

Simple wisdom might be fine for Dust Bowl living, but not for a sophisticated woman of the world. And that's what Abigail aimed to be. Four years in the real world taught her that success is measured in job titles and social status. God didn't even enter the real world equation.

Her eye-opening meeting with Dean Henderson four years ago was the beginning of a long line of lessons on real life. There had been dozens of lessons during her years at college from friends, magazines, and television, even some from professors. Each lesson drew the same conclusions. Being a success, a person with position, money, and prestige was everything. And Abigail knew that there were no successes in Dust Bowl.

She loved her father, but this time he was wrong.

That Sunday morning, it seemed to Abigail the entire town knew about her job, and everyone had something to say about it.

After making his opening remarks and announcements from the pulpit during Sunday worship, Pastor Johnson singled her out. "It's good to see our Abby back from college this morning."

He beamed down at Abigail as every eye in the crowded sanctuary homed in on her. "We're all praying the Lord's direction for you, Abby. That He'll lead you right back to Dust Bowl, to the folks who love you."

Abigail smiled politely at the nodding congregation, wondering if anything could be worse than having a whole room of well-meaning friends praying against you.

Following the service, there was a covered dish dinner in the fellowship hall. Abigail hoped the topic of her job wouldn't come up and that she could eat her meal in peace.

"Pretty young girl like yourself could get lost in the big city," Emma Bankston pronounced with a wag of her head as she placed two big pieces of crispy fried chicken on Abigail's plate and passed it down.

Darlene Evans accepted the plate with a nod of agreement. "Television news is chock full of stories of good people that have lost their way in the evils of the world." She added a big scoop of potato salad to the plate and handed it along.

The elderly spinster twins, BettiLou and SaraBeth Strade, managed the end of the serving line. BettiLou, the more sweet-tempered of the two, spooned a healthy serving of green beans onto the only vacant space on the plate. "No matter what any-one says, I don't believe you've lost your mind, what with want-ing to move to the big city and all." She leaned toward Abigail to confide, "I s'pect it's just a case of growing pains. It'll pass." She passed the plate across the table into Abigail's hands.

"And just what do you remember about growing pains?" SaraBeth snapped at her sister. Without waiting for a reply, she spun around to demand of Abigail, "Blueberry or apple?"

"Blueberry, please."

SaraBeth handed her a separate plastic plate with a large slice of homemade pie. "Trust me. You won't last out the year." Hav-ing made her dire prediction, she smiled a sweet grandmotherly smile at Abigail. "Enjoy your lunch, dear."

Abigail spied an empty spot between her brother Phillip and Jarred and hurried to their table to take refuge.

"You fellas mind if I sit here?"

Jarred stood to take the plates from her. "Have a seat, Abby. We were just talking about you."

She lowered herself onto the metal folding chair. "Let me guess. Did it have something to do with my new job?"

"Lighten up, Abby," Phillip admonished her with a wave of his fork. "Folks are just concerned about you. They don't want to see you make a mistake."

Phillip's chastening was the last straw. "Mistake!" Her voice shook with suppressed anger. "The only mistake I made was to be born in a one-horse hick town like Dust Bowl!" She stood up, pushing back her chair with her legs. "Just because you're satisfied to be nothing," she railed at him, "wasting your life in this miserable little town, doesn't mean I should be condemned to do so too."

Jarred reached for her hand, trying to coax her back into her chair, but Abigail was beyond consolation. "I'm going to make something of myself!" she announced, her gaze sweeping all the stunned occupants of the long rectangular table. "And none of you can stop me!"

Phillip put a finger to his lips, "Sit down, Abby. You need—"

"I don't need anything from you or anyone!" She felt like a complete fool standing at the table with tears streaming down her cheeks, screaming like an idiot at her poor bewildered brother, but she couldn't seem to stop.

"As far as I'm concerned, Dust Bowl is history. If you want to see me, you can look for me on the society page of the *Herald*." Having directed that to the table at large, she turned and marched from the room.

ર

Abigail set her fork down and pushed the lasagna away. The vivid year-old memory spoiled her appetite, filling her empty stomach with dread. What in the world was she thinking when she agreed to go back to Dust Bowl?

five

Seated at her desk the following morning, Abigail picked up the stack of letters addressed to the Notebook and began to sort through them. As Notebook Coordinator, her job was to compile a list of community events for the upcoming week from the mail she received, organize it into a calendar format, and have it ready for publication in Saturday morning's paper.

Other than the few judgment calls she was required to make as to whether a mailed submission was appropriate for the paper, Abigail knew the average chimpanzee could perform her job effortlessly.

It was a far cry from the coveted place on the staff of the society page. Her thoughts wandered back to her Monday morning interview a year ago.

❧

"Good morning, Mr. Robinson. Hope I'm not too early." Abigail had bounded into his office, too excited to notice his somber expression.

"Have a seat, Ms. Bradley."

Something in his tone of voice alerted her to the gravity of the situation. She swallowed hard. "Is there a problem?" she asked as she lowered herself into the proffered chair. "Did I get the job?"

"I've got a job for you, Ms. Bradley, but I'm afraid it's not in the society section."

"They. . .they didn't want me?" Abigail stammered.

Mr. Robinson's face softened. "It's not that. Another applicant had, uh, better credentials for a society reporter." He folded his hands on his desk. "I am, however, prepared to offer you a job in the Notebook. Your skills and writing ability should—"

Abigail quit listening beyond the part where he said the society page job went to somebody else. *Someone else had better credentials. . .* She knew what that meant. No doubt the other applicant didn't hail from a backward town like Dust Bowl. It confirmed what Dean Henderson said: her small town background was a liability.

She felt sick. This couldn't be happening. She'd counted on getting the job. She needed it. The society page had meant so much more than a job to Abigail. It might be her only opportunity to make something of herself.

She accepted the position in Notebook from Mr. Robinson that day, not because she wanted it, but to save face. She *had* to work for the paper in some capacity. After all, she'd bragged to everyone she was a reporter for the *Herald*. Maybe nobody in Dust Bowl would find out the truth.

ন্ধ

Lurline appeared, stirring Abigail from her memories by waving two cups over the top of her cubicle. "Break time."

Abigail glanced up at the clock on the wall and smiled. "It's eight-fifteen, Lurline. We've only been working for fifteen minutes."

Lurline set the cups on Abigail's desk and shrugged unrepentantly. "No sense in working ourselves to death."

Abigail relented and logged off her program. "Things must be slow in Obituaries today."

"Heavens no, people are always dying to get into print."

Abigail groaned. "Honestly! I don't know how you can kid about stuff like that. It's so creepy."

"Naw," Lurline pushed back in her chair and ran a hand through her unruly orange curls. "Death's not creepy. It's a part of life— a natural occurrence. I consider my job in Obituaries to be one of a historian. Nothing creepy about that."

Abigail propped her elbows on the desk and rested her chin in her hands. "I hadn't thought about it that way before. I mean about obituaries being history." She stared off into space. "Do you realize my whole life could be reduced down to an inch by inch column in the *Herald*."

"It won't. Don't you see?" Lurline took a draught from her cup. "You're gonna make something of yourself, just like you've always said you would. You don't think important folks get a puny obituary do you? Heavens no! It takes almost a half page just to list all the endowments they've bestowed."

"Ironic, isn't it?" Abigail said, idly tracing the rim of her cup with her fingertip. "Successful people get special treatment even when they're dead!"

"Don't you worry. Once you're a full-fledged reporter, and hobnobbing with Edward and his friends, you'll be joining the ranks of successful people in no time."

Abigail shook her head. "Don't be too sure. Mr. Robinson hasn't mentioned anything else about me working as a reporter since I submitted the stock show results, and I haven't heard a word from Edward since our one and only date."

"I'm not worried. I've got faith in you. Say, not to change the subject, but speaking of the stock show brings up a critical issue. Where does Dimples fit in?"

Abigail laughed. "You must mean Jarred."

Lurline nodded. "That's the one. The cowboy type with the grin."

"Jarred's just a friend, Lurline."

"Mighty fine-looking friend." Lurline wiggled her eyebrows suggestively.

Abigail ignored the remark and the expression. "Technically, Jarred is my brother Phillip's friend. I used to tag along with them, whenever they'd let me."

Lurline's eyes narrowed suspiciously. "Sounds to me like it's *your* friendship he's after now. I mean, it wasn't your brother he invited to the stock show."

Abigail shrugged. "That's just because I happened to run in to him. It was no big deal. He knew I had a date. He was the one that suggested I bring Edward along."

"I don't know, Abigail. I've got a bad feeling about him. You can't get mixed up with Jarred. Falling for him could ruin everything we've worked for."

Abigail shook her head slowly and heaved a long-suffering sigh. "You're not listening to me, Lurline. It's not like that between Jarred and me. He thinks of me like a kid sister."

Lurline snorted and rolled her eyes.

"No really, I mean it. He's always kind of looked after me. It's like he helped raise me. He checked my homework, warded off bullies, that sort of thing. He even stopped by the house to meet my dates. It was always real casual, like he just happened to drop by to talk to my brother, but I could tell he was checking them out."

Abigail leaned closer to confide. "I remember one particular time, when I was a junior in high school, I had a date to the movies with a senior, Arthur Beemur. After the show, he drove me to Possum Point, Dust Bowl's favorite spot for sparking. Just as Arthur wrapped his arm around my shoulders I happened to glance out the window. Who do you suppose I saw marching up to the car?"

"Jarred?" Lurline gasped.

Abigail nodded. "Somehow he'd gotten wind of Arthur's plans and he was hopping mad. He jerked old Arthur out of the car so fast I thought he was going to get whiplash."

"That's about the most romantic thing I've ever heard," Lurline said with a dreamy sigh. "Jarred charged up like a knight in shining armor to protect your honor."

"Mercy no, Lurline, you've missed the whole point!" Abigail cried in exasperation. "That's not romance. That's brotherly."

She frowned into Lurline's disbelieving look. "You wouldn't have thought it was too romantic if you'd have been there when Jarred loaded me into his truck and took me home, lecturing me the whole time on how I was supposed to save my kisses for the man I'll marry."

"He was really mad, huh?"

Abigail grew thoughtful. "No," she said, remembering the look on Jarred's face as he stood with her at the front door of her parents' house that night. "I wouldn't say mad. More sad, I think."

The memory was so strong Lurline's presence was temporarily forgotten. "The porch light was on when we got home," Abigail said, speaking her thoughts aloud. "We were standing so close I could see his eyes really well. I remember thinking they looked strange."

Abigail glanced over to her friend as if seeing her for the first time. "I guess you'd have to know Jarred's eyes to understand what I mean," she explained. "He has wonderful eyes." Her mouth curved into an unconscious smile as she said, "They're big and a real deep brown and they always seem to sparkle, like he knows something funny—but they weren't sparkling that night. He put a fingertip to my lips and whispered, 'Please wait.' Then he left."

"Wow." Lurline said on a long sigh.

It had been years since Abigail thought about that night. She'd forgotten how deeply it had touched her. "The point is," she said, rubbing her upper arms vigorously to erase the mysterious bumps that suddenly appeared with a chill. "Jarred was looking after me. Like a big brother. The only thing between Jarred and me is friendship."

Lurline folded her long arms across her chest and raised a skeptical brow. "And you're telling me you've never had a crush on Jarred."

"I never said that." Abigail felt her face flush with the honest confession. "Of course I had a crush on him."

She met Lurline's smug look with a narrowed gaze. "Now don't give me that look, Lurline. I know what you're thinking and you're wrong. Everybody had a crush on Jarred. He's just a lovable kind of guy."

Lurline set the trap, "Not to mention the dimples."

Abigail took the bait. "Yeah, the dimples," she sighed.

"That explains it."

Abigail didn't like the gleam she suddenly noticed in Lurline's eyes. "Explains what?"

"The goose bumps I saw on your arm after Dimples left. He must have kissed you," she finished smoothly.

The statement caught Abigail off guard. "Yes, he did," she answered matter-of-factly. Her eyes widened in alarm. "Now wait just a minute," she protested. "It was just a peck. A *brotherly* peck! On my forehead. That doesn't count as a kiss."

Lurline seemed to be mulling it over. "I wouldn't think so. A peck is just a peck, certainly not a kiss. But the goose bumps. . ." Her voice trailed off. She set her empty cup on the desk and got to her feet. "Break's over. Gotta get back to work." She gave a distracted wave and disappeared down the hall.

Abigail shook her head ruefully. "What an imagination that girl has. Making such a big deal about a little thing like goose bumps."

❧

The phone at her elbow jangled sometime later, interrupting her typing. "Notebook, Bradley speaking."

"Abigail? This is Edward Winters."

Abigail smiled. He didn't need to identify himself to her. His speech had a distinctively refined, slightly nasal manner that no other caller could duplicate. "Hi, Edward." She tried to sound casual. "What can I do for you?"

"You can forgive me for calling so late and accept my invitation to dinner on Saturday night."

"Saturday night?"

"I know it's late notice," Edward apologized. "I thought I would be out on the West Coast for the weekend and I only just found out those plans have been canceled. I'd love to see you."

"Saturday would be fine, Edward."

"That's great. I thought we might try Hubert's, downtown. Can I pick you up around seven?"

"Sure. I'll be ready at seven."

Abigail hung up the phone with a grin. Hubert's was an exclusive restaurant she'd read about in all of Lurline's gossip magazines. The kind of place where the patrons list read like a page from *Who's Who in Oklahoma Society*. Wait till Lurline heard about this. That should take her one-track mind off goose bumps and Jarred!

six

Queen Elizabeth didn't have it anything better than this. Valets to park cars, doormen to open doors, dignified maitre d's in midnight black tuxedos to escort patrons to tables, and waiters to cater to their every whim. Hubert's was truly a first class place.

Once they were seated at a cozy table near the center of the room, Abigail noted with pride that every person in Hubert's, whether staff or patron, recognized Edward and called him by name. Now *that* was being successful.

She clutched the menu in her hands, too excited to focus on the entrées. She could almost swear the hand-lettered parchment menu was housed in a real leather cover. Wow. One surely didn't find this kind of luxury back in Dust Bowl.

Abigail was further impressed to find the cloth covering the table was actually a lavish two layers of real linen, a creamy white one angled on top to expose the hunter green layer underneath. Abigail fingered the fine fabric, wondering vaguely if they had to change both layers between patrons. Such extravagance.

She watched as light flickered and danced off the crystal vase holding a solitary white rose. Pure elegance. Abigail wished Lurline could be there to see this.

She glanced back at the menu. Everything looked so delicious it was difficult to decide. She thought the shrimp might be nice. It had been a long time since she'd eaten seafood. On the other hand, a nice thick filet sounded good.

Her gaze wandered to the right side of the page, thinking she would use the price to break the tie. The good manners instilled in her since childhood dictated one did not order the most expensive thing on the menu. After her many indiscretions at the stock show, she was more determined than ever to impress Edward with her polished upbringing.

To her surprise, the right column was blank. No prices. No writing at all. She rolled her eyes in despair. Just her luck that the person who had drawn up her menu was in such a hurry he forgot to pen them in.

She supposed she could ask to see Edward's menu, but that

might be too obvious. Terrific. Now how would she know which entrée was lower priced? How could she demonstrate her worldly sophistication to Edward? The telltale throbbing in her head indicated she'd need the small packet of aspirin tucked in her evening bag.

She was discreetly unwrapping the aspirin as she studied over the list of entrées again when a solution presented itself. Chicken! Chicken was always inexpensive. She tucked the packet back inside the evening bag and set it aside. Perhaps she wouldn't need the aspirin after all.

"Have you made a decision, Miss?"

Abigail smiled triumphantly at the waiter. "Yes. I'd like the Chicken a la Hubert, please."

Edward leaned toward her. "Their steaks are phenomenal here," he said. "Are you sure you wouldn't like to reconsider?"

"No!" she answered quickly. Thinking her response to be too abrupt she added, "No thanks, chicken for me." That singsong reply sounded a bit silly so she supplemented it with an additional explanation in an overly loud voice, "I like chicken. *Love* it, actually."

The waiter's brow arched slightly before he turned to Edward. "And you, Mr. Winters?"

"Steak, please. Medium rare."

After the waiter disappeared, Edward said. "I hope you don't think I was criticizing your selection. Chicken a la Hubert is really quite delicious."

Abigail felt so foolish. Sophisticated people simply did not become emotional about entrées.

Perhaps she should try to explain.

A plausible explanation in the form of a little white lie manifested itself almost immediately. "I uh, I'm trying to be more fat-conscious—you know, less red meat."

Edward nodded approvingly. "So speaks the American people." He rested his elbows on the table and steepled his long fingers. "In fact, in a recent move to diversify some of my holdings, I bought heavily into poultry interests. Frankly, chicken makes a great investment."

"But lousy pets."

Edward looked puzzled. "I'm sorry?"

Abigail's eyes widened in horror. The comment slipped out before she gave it a thought and now it was too late to take it back. *You can take the girl out of Dust Bowl, but you can't take the Dust Bowl out of the girl.* Her stomach turned as she repeated herself in a self-conscious whisper, "I said chickens make lousy pets."

At Edward's raised brow she felt the need to elaborate. "I have extensive experience with both hens and roosters of various breeds, and I can state unequivocally, chickens make lousy pets."

Edward studied her with interest. At least, it appeared to be interest, the way he regarded her with an unblinking gaze. Abigail was so relieved that with the change of topic he seemed to have forgotten her awkwardness with the waiter that she cheerfully volunteered, "I've been pecked hundreds of times."

Her face sobered. "Of course, it's difficult to blame them."

"Is it?"

Abigail's head bobbed. "Oh sure. I have my own theory." She leaned forward to explain, "I think chickens are ill-tempered because they have an inherent sense about what is to become of them."

"And that is?" The bewildered look was back on Edward's face.

Abigail shrugged matter-of-factly. "Dinner, of course. We ate them."

Edward said nothing. For a full minute, he simply stared.

Abigail became alarmed. *What have I said now?* Without delay she withdrew two aspirin tablets from her bag and popped them into her mouth.

Suddenly, Edward began to chuckle. "Abigail, you are priceless," he said with a grin, placing his smooth hands over hers. "What a sense of humor you have."

Abigail wasn't certain what she'd said that was funny but she returned his smile.

It was at that moment, when they were holding hands and smiling at one another, that Suzanne Masters from the *Herald* appeared beside the table. Abigail steeled herself for the customary caustic blow.

Suzanne took a moment to absorb what she was seeing before speaking. "Abigail? Abigail Bradley? It's so good to see you," she gushed. "How are you?"

Abigail was aghast. Suzanne Masters was actually smiling at her. It didn't take long to figure out her motivation.

"Won't you introduce me to your friend?"

Abigail smiled coolly. "Edward Winters, I'd like you to meet Suzanne Masters."

Edward got to his feet. "Suzanne." He shook her hand. "Good to meet you."

"What a pleasure it is to meet you. I've heard so much about you. My father is well acquainted with your family. Perhaps you've heard of him. Richard Masters?"

Edward nodded. "Yes, I know your father."

Suzanne giggled. "Isn't it a small world."

Abigail rolled her eyes in disgust. The woman was making an idiot of herself.

Fortunately, the waiter arrived. "Oh look, Edward," Abigail said, "our salads are here." She directed her next statement to Suzanne. "I'm famished."

Taking the not-so-subtle hint, Suzanne reluctantly excused herself leaving them to their meal.

Conversation over dinner was light with Edward doing most of the talking. Abigail was on her guard now. She knew it wasn't safe to relax, that a bit of Dust Bowl could spring out of her mouth without warning. Luckily, Edward seemed content to talk about himself.

"Everything was delicious, Edward." Abigail dabbed the corners of her mouth with her linen napkin before laying it on the table beside her dessert plate. "Thank you so much for bringing me here."

"I'm glad you enjoyed it." He pushed up the sleeve of his jacket to check his watch. "It's still early. Would you like to drop by the club for a while?"

Hubert's and the club too? Abigail could scarcely believe her good fortune. Lurline would flip! "I'd love to."

Edward signed the check and the two of them headed for the door, with Edward pausing frequently to greet an acquaintance.

Abigail sighed. He was truly an important person. A real success.

The same thought struck her an hour later. She was seated on a sumptuous leather couch, Edward by her side, surrounded by a host of elegant people. Abigail said little, content to be an observer. These were the beautiful people of Oklahoma society, the jet-setters, the elite. For Abigail, this was a dream come true.

"Aren't you going to introduce us to your friend, Edward?" The question came from an unidentified person in the cluster of people surrounding them.

Edward placed a possessive arm around Abigail's shoulder. "Meet Abigail Bradley."

As Edward was drawn aside into a conversation with an acquaintance, a sleek woman with exotic dark eyes approached Abigail. "Why don't you tell us about yourself, Abigail." The request sounded more like a challenge than a stab at polite conversation.

Abigail cringed inwardly. She didn't want to draw attention to herself. She was nothing compared to these people. A square peg. "There isn't much to tell, I'm afraid." She lifted her shoulders into a negligent shrug, hoping attention would be directed elsewhere.

"Don't be shy, Abigail. We don't bite." The woman smiled at her companions. "We're just curious, that's all. We're always interested in Edward's friends. So tell me, where are you from? What do you do?" the woman pressed closer. "What does your father do?"

A deafening quiet settled over the room, and it seemed to Abigail that every eye was leveled on her. Her heart ground to a halt and a hard knot of dread settled into the pit of her stomach.

This was the moment of truth. Did she confess to the glittering crowd that she was a Dust Bowl girl? That revelation would certainly sound the social death knell. And what would they think about her father's occupation—the proud owner of a rusty old two-pump gas station back home? She doubted her job at the paper could hold a candle to their positions.

The crowd waited. Abigail summoned a bright smile. "I'm from a small town west of here. It's so small it doesn't even rate a dot on the map." She held up her hand to illustrate, her thumb and index finger a scant inch apart. Several people chuckled and she felt a bit more confident.

"I escaped to the city after graduating from college and now I work at the *Herald*." She shrugged again. "Like I said, there's nothing newsworthy about me."

A different woman, this one short with frosted blond hair, looked genuinely impressed. "The *Herald?* How exciting."

"What does your family do?"

Abigail raised her eyes to the speaker, the same exotic woman who had begun the interrogation. She took a deep breath. "My family? Well—uh, my daddy is in—he's in oil." She hoped the others couldn't hear her screaming conscience. It seemed to her that it took an awful lot of lies to make something of oneself.

A satisfied murmur of approval rose from the crowd. Her brief, vague, and admittedly misleading answers seemed to appease the appetite of the crowd and the conversation drifted to another topic of interest. Even the dark-eyed woman appeared content.

Abigail sighed in relief. She passed the test. Nobody noticed she wasn't one of them. She could relax. Almost.

It was nearly two A.M. when Edward pulled his English two-seater sports car into her driveway. "I've had a great time tonight, Abigail," he said as he turned off the engine.

"Me too," Abigail said sleepily. "Thanks for dinner and introducing me to your friends at the club."

"I've got tickets for the ballet on Thursday night. Would you be interested in going?"

"The ballet?" Abigail knew nothing about ballet. Except that successful people patronized the arts. "I'd love to."

Edward smiled. "Good. It's all settled then. And maybe we can catch a show over the weekend."

"Next weekend?" Abigail shook her head. "I'm sorry. I'm going out of town."

"Oh?"

"I've agreed to help Jarred decorate his new house."

"I should have known."

"Known what?" Surely he didn't believe as Lurline did that somehow Jarred and Abigail were romantically inclined.

"That a wonderful woman like you would take time out of her busy schedule and spend it with the underprivileged."

She bristled at the reference to her friend. "I'm not sure the term underprivileged applies to Jarred. I hear he's doing very well."

He patted her hand soothingly. "Not financially underprivileged. Culturally. Anyway, I'm proud of you."

The conversation had taken a decidedly uncomfortable turn. Abigail wasn't certain why she'd agreed to go back home, but she knew it wasn't to help the underprivileged. "I guess I better run in."

Edward walked her to the door and waited as she unlocked it. "Goodnight, Abigail." He bent to kiss her. Abigail raised her lips to his, determined that this time she would pay close attention. She wanted to prove to Lurline once and for all that her reaction to Jarred's kisses meant nothing.

His mouth was pleasantly warm on hers and her shoulders felt warm where his hands rested. After a few seconds of contact he pulled away. "Goodnight, Abigail. Sleep well."

"Goodnight, Edward." She stepped inside the door and closed it behind her. Immediately, she raised her arm to the light for examination.

Nothing. The skin was as smooth as silk.

seven

Lurline spied Abigail slumped dejectedly behind her desk and stated the obvious. "You haven't left yet, huh?"

Abigail didn't look up. "Naw, not yet."

"Hey, pal," Lurline said softly. "If you're going to go, you'd best be gettin' on. It's getting late, almost seven and you have a two and a half hour drive ahead of you."

Abigail heaved a heavy sigh. "Yeah, I know."

Lurline placed a comforting hand on her shoulder. "Abigail, would it help any if I came with you? I could, you know. I'm not doing anything special this weekend." She grinned. "Of course, that's not exactly headline news. I never do anything on weekends."

Abigail lifted her gaze to her friend and a slow smile of appreciation spread across her face. "Thanks for the offer, but I think I'd better go it alone."

"You could always cancel," Lurline offered. "You know, call Dimples and tell him you're tied up with work."

Abigail seriously considered the option one last time before shaking her head. "No," she said. "I'm going."

Both women fell silent. The only sound in the nearly deserted office was the hum of the fluorescent lights overhead.

"Oh well," Lurline tried for optimism. "Maybe it won't be as bad as you think."

Abigail looked hopefully at her friend.

"Maybe the good people of Dust Bowl have forgotten all about you calling their beloved city 'a miserable, one-horse hick town.' "

Abigail's brow shot up in disbelief.

"You're right." Lurline lifted her hands in concession. "People tend to remember stuff like that, don't they?"

"I'm afraid so."

Another long pause.

"So what are you going to do?"

Good question, Abigail thought miserably, *what am I going to do? Why in the world am I subjecting myself to this torture?* Jarred and his dimples.

Suddenly, she sat up straight in her chair with new determination. "I'm going to stop by Jarred's place tomorrow morning, like I promised. I figure he's got things pretty much together—he probably just needs me to help with basic furniture arrangement and hanging pictures. Stuff like that."

"Sounds easy enough."

"It will be," Abigail declared with more force than conviction. She gathered her purse in her arms. "Okay, I'm ready." She flashed a pained grin. "At least, I'm as ready as I'll ever be."

Lurline slapped her companionably on the back. "That'a girl."

They walked out together to the employee parking lot. "Have a safe trip, Abigail," Lurline called, swinging open the door of her aging sedan. "I want to hear all about it on Monday."

"Thanks, Lurline," she said as Lurline rolled down her window. "You're the best."

The trip home went smoothly. Her little red car purred along the long black stretches of highway, carrying her out of the chaotic downtown traffic to the wide open spaces of the Oklahoma countryside. She could almost feel the stress roll off her shoulders.

Abigail used the time to bolster her sagging confidence. "It's not going to be so bad," she told herself. "After all, it's not like I haven't been back home since the big scene."

That part was true. She'd traveled back to Dust Bowl four times over the last year. Once each for her mother's, brother's, and father's birthdays, and once for Christmas.

Each visit was deliberately brief—less than twenty-four hours. She would arrive early enough to celebrate the event over dinner with her family and would depart shortly after breakfast the following morning.

The quick in and outs spared her the embarrassment of running into anyone who may have witnessed her outburst at the covered dish supper and also eliminated any opportunities for someone to ask questions about her job at the paper.

Abigail sighed. What an awkward mess she'd gotten herself into. There didn't seem to be a lot of truth involved in the business of becoming a success.

It was a little before ten when Abigail spotted the familiar sign up ahead. WELCOME TO DUST BOWL. Seeing the green metal sign, riddled with bullet holes, brought back a flood of memories. Abigail grinned.

Five long years ago she'd been a senior at Dust Bowl High. After the commencement ceremonies the entire graduating class, all seventeen of them, loaded into pickup trucks and drove out to the edge of town to shoot at the sign just as the graduating seniors had done for decades.

Abigail didn't know which class initiated the odd ritual, but it stuck, becoming a rite of passage for future classes. The city fathers took the vandalism in stride and an ongoing fund was established to replace the sign when it became illegible—shot to tatters.

She could still remember how delighted she had been when Jarred and Phillip offered to drive her out to the city limits that night. Being escorted by two older men was a incredible status boost, even if one them was her brother. The threesome had watched together as each of her classmates took their shots.

"Your turn, Abby." Clovis Tate handed her the rifle. Abigail reluctantly accepted the gun and held it up against her shoulder as she had seen the others do.

The crowd was silent as she took her time lining up the sign in her sights. They erupted into cheers as she squeezed the trigger, then groaned when it was clear she'd missed the target completely.

"Come on, Abby," Clovis entreated. "You can do better than that."

Abigail shook her head and lowered the rifle with trembling hands. "I'm not very good with guns," she confessed. "Someone else can have my turn."

The crowd wasn't having any part of it. "It's tradition. We stay till she hits it," rose the cry.

Abigail turned to Jarred and Phillip, a desperate plea for help written across her face. Jarred reacted immediately. "If it's all the same with you," he joked, "I'd like to get home before sunrise. Mind if I offer a little assistance?"

She would never forget her rush of relief as he stepped forward. Jarred was there. Everything would be all right. He stood behind her, gently turning her toward the sign. With his strong arms around her, his hands covering hers, he lifted the gun, sighted the sign, and fired several shots.

The crowd was cheering again, but her attention was focused entirely on the man holding her in his arms. That intimate moment brought with it a strange new awareness of her childhood friend. His special soapy-clean scent, the warmth of his breath on her neck, and the strong solid feel of his chest combined to send mysteriously delicious shivers up her spine.

She'd long forgotten the precise spot their bullets struck the target, but she had a clear memory to this day of how wonderful it felt to be held in his arms.

All too quickly he had moved away, fading back into the crowd of spectators. The ritual completed, her classmates swarmed around her offering congratulations and best wishes. Her gaze had swept beyond them, seeking out Jarred to find him and thank him.

Their eyes met and for a moment it had seemed to Abigail that they were the only two people in the world. She mouthed her thanks to him, knowing full well he wouldn't be able to hear her above the din. He winked in acknowledgment and his teeth flashed in a broad grin. And the dimples…

Abigail swung her car into her parents' driveway and shut off the engine. The house was dark, her mom and dad had obviously retired for the evening. She smiled. There was no reason to stay up past nine o'clock in Dust Bowl.

When she got to the front door she transferred her suitcase from her right to her left hand and tried the knob. It opened easily, just as she expected. She'd never been able to convince her parents to lock the doors.

"Don't be silly," they'd say. "We haven't any crime in Dust Bowl." *Of course not,* she thought rather snippishly, *there's nothing in Dust Bowl worth stealing.*

She stepped inside and quietly closed the door behind her. She moved carefully through the pitch black living room and down the dark hall. She paused at her parents' door. The rhythmic breathing was a good indication they'd been asleep for some time.

She continued down the hall to her bedroom and flipped on

the light. Everything was the same in her small room. It was as though time stood still.

Ribbons won during her years of participation in 4H decorated the walls. The slightly faded pink gingham bedspread she'd gotten in seventh grade still covered her twin size bed. A favorite teddy bear reclined against the pillow as if awaiting her return.

Abigail put her things away, changed into pajamas, slipped in between the crisp sheets, and felt herself dropping off instantly—unlike in the city where she would often lay in bed an hour or two courting sleep.

In spite of her misgivings about coming home, she was strangely peaceful. Her last conscious thought before oblivion was of Jarred. And his dimples.

ta

Abigail's dreams, a pleasant collage of memories, were superimposed with the smell of frying bacon. She resisted the olfactory pull toward consciousness by rolling onto her side and hiking her covers up over her shoulders.

The delicious aroma proved more tenacious than Abigail's willpower and she reluctantly opened her eyes to the new day. She focused slowly on the familiar trappings of her old room—the desk with her dilapidated typewriter, freshly starched curtains hanging in the window, the clock radio on the nightstand. Her eyes came to rest on the clock. She read the time, blinked hard and read it again. *Six-thirty? This is Dust Bowl. Folks here get up with the sun, weekday or weekend.*

It did seem odd that her parents started breakfast without her. They usually fixed it as a family when she was at home. Abigail's eyes flew open with the realization she had never called them to say she was coming. Unless they happened to look out the living room window and see her car parked outside, they would have no idea she was there.

A spark of mischief lit her eyes. She'd sneak down the hall and surprise them.

She scrambled out of bed, grabbing her robe from the closet and pulling it on over her pajamas on her way out of the room. She stifled a delighted giggle of anticipation as she tiptoed down the hall toward the kitchen. She vetoed the fleeting thought that she should take an extra minute to brush her hair, the thrill of the ambush beckoning her onward.

Abigail paused just outside the doorway of the kitchen for a split second, silently congratulating herself on her brilliant scheme. *They are really going to be surprised,* she thought smugly.

On the silent count of three she burst into the kitchen flailing her arms and shouting, "Surprise! I'm home! I'm home!"

As it turned out, the surprise was on her.

Her father calmly lowered the newspaper he was reading to say, "Well looky here, Momma. Look what the cat drug in!"

The upraised section of newspaper beside her father dipped slightly to reveal a grinning Jarred, two large dents cutting his tanned cheeks. "Morning, Abby, honey. Welcome home."

Abigail wanted to drop through the floor.

"Abby! What a wonderful surprise!" Her mother set her spatula on the counter and embraced her daughter warmly. "Jarred told us you were coming."

Although there was no censure in her voice, Abigail felt the need to explain. "I'm sorry I didn't call, Mom. I got tied up—" Another lie.

"It's no matter, darlin'. We're just glad you're here." Her mom hugged her again. "Go sit down now, and I'll serve up breakfast."

Abigail dropped a kiss on her father's head before obediently taking her place at the table across from Jarred. She sincerely regretted her decision to hurry into the kitchen without peeking into a mirror.

Her hand stole up to smooth her sleep-tossed tresses as best she could, but she knew the effort was futile. From what she could feel, a significant portion of her hair stood straight up from her scalp. To make matters worse, Jarred was smiling broadly, looking like a million dollars, just as she suspected he would.

Her mother came to the table with a big bowl of scrambled eggs in one hand and a platter of bacon in the other. Before she sat down she added a bowl of steaming grits, a plate stacked high with buttered toast, and a basket of her famous blueberry muffins.

Her father asked a blessing on the food. "Lord, bless this food to the nourishment of our bodies. And thank You for this special time with our Abby. In Jesus' name I pray. Amen."

Abigail's self-consciousness faded quickly in the comfortable atmosphere of the cozy kitchen. In no time at all she was eating with a ferocious appetite and trading quips with Jarred and her parents.

"Jarred tells us you're going to help out at his place," her father said between bites.

Abigail nodded. "I'm not too sure I can be of much good, but he's convinced he needs me to help decorate."

Her mother looked perplexed. "Decorate? Isn't it a mite early—"

Abigail missed the quelling look her father shot her mother. "I think it's a great idea, Abby," he interrupted. "You always did have a special way with fixing things up."

"She's a whiz," Jarred added, favoring Abigail with a warm smile. "Rumor has it, she can make something from nothing."

"Strikes me those skills are gonna come in mighty handy," her mother mumbled.

Her father must have seen the question form in Abigail's eyes. "So how's work?" he asked, deliberately changing the subject. "Paper keeping you busy?"

Abigail felt a warm flush creep across her cheeks. Work was a topic she didn't want to discuss. She wished she'd been honest with her parents from the beginning. She should have confessed she didn't get the society job and that she was nothing more than a clerk in Notebook. The lies had gone on so long now, she couldn't make herself recant.

"Very busy," she answered halfheartedly.

"Folks around here are mighty proud of our girl making good in the big city. Why I believe nearly everybody in Dust Bowl has started taking the *Herald*."

"True enough," her mother agreed. "Fact is, business was so good, Elmer had to add a new carrier to the paper route."

Her father's eyes glowed with pride. "I bet your mother and I get at least a call a day, somebody telling us what a fine job you're doing on the society page."

Abigail's appetite died a swift death. She was so mortified by the enormity of her deceit, she couldn't raise her eyes from her plate to meet those of her family. She settled for shifting the food from one side of the plate to the other with her fork.

Her mother noticed. "Abby, honey, you're not finished already are you? You haven't even tasted one of my blueberry muffins."

"I'm not actually working on the society page." Abigal blurted the truth. "I do something else at the paper." She turned to Jarred, eager for an escape. "If you'll give me thirty minutes to shower and dress, we can be on our way."

"It's a deal." He winked at her before turning his attention back to her mother. "Now, Mrs. Bradley, if you're anxious to get rid of those muffins I believe I could be enticed to eat another."

Abigail took a quick shower and blow-dried her hair into a soft bob. She took extra time with her grooming hoping to erase the memory of her first appearance that morning.

From her closet she chose a pair of faded jeans and a chambray shirt. *Not glamorous*, she thought, studying her reflection in the mirror, *but very practical for moving furniture*. She slipped into a pair of comfortable sneakers and headed back for the kitchen.

Jarred gave a low whistle of appreciation as she reentered the room. "Mercy, Abby!" he declared, rising to his feet, "you clean up real nice." He walked over to her and wrapped a well-muscled arm around her shoulder. "Mmmm," he teased as he buried his face in her hair and inhaled deeply, "you smell purty, too."

She glanced up to deliver a light-hearted response when his brown eyes took hers captive. "Now how in the world am I gonna concentrate on my work," he asked, his voice a velvety whisper, "when I've got a beautiful woman distracting me?"

Abigail felt her knees wobble and an odd little shiver creep up her spine as she stared into the depths of Jarred's eyes. For a suspended moment, she couldn't draw a breath.

The instant eye contact was broken and her heart slowed to resume its natural rhythm, she discounted the breathless sensation as meaningless and assured herself the thrill she felt was simply satisfaction that he finally recognized her as an adult.

Jarred and Abigail had been friends since before she could walk. Because she was six years younger than Jarred and her brother, Phillip, they had always considered her a kid. Even when she was in college they treated her like a child. But today he called her a woman.

"Mrs. Bradley, thanks so much for the fine breakfast," Jarred said with a broad grin. "If it's all right with you folks, I think we'll be on our way."

"You kids have a nice time—decorating."

Outside, Jarred held the truck door open for Abigail and she slid onto the seat. She was settled inside and he had started the truck when she suddenly remembered her aspirin. "Wait, Jarred!" she exclaimed. "I forgot something." She hopped out of the truck and ran up the driveway to her car, scooped up the new bottle of aspirin, and hurried back to the waiting truck.

"Thanks," she said as she climbed in and pulled the door shut. "I'll need this."

"A quart of aspirin?" he asked with a mixture of humor and alarm.

"It's not a quart, silly," she corrected, holding up the bottle for his inspection. "It's an economy size bottle. Trust me," she laughed, "with as many headaches as I get, I need to buy in bulk."

Jarred apparently failed to see the humor in her remark. He shifted the truck into park and turned to stare at her, concern etched across his face. "I didn't know you had a lot of headaches."

Abigail nodded. "Oh sure, at least one a day. One big one." She shrugged negligently. "One of the hazards of life in the big city."

"Sounds serious."

Abigail shook her head. "Not according to the doctor. He assured me it's just one of the side effects of stress."

Jarred was visibly relieved. He shifted the truck into reverse and eased it down the driveway and into the street. "You know, honey, you've got a much better way to deal with stress than aspirin."

"I do?"

"Sure. There's a prescription in the Bible. It tells us not to worry about anything and to pray about everything. The promised result is peace."

Abigail studied his strong profile closely to determine if he was actually serious. Not that she should be surprised. After all, he was of the same school as her father. They firmly believed faith in God and consistent Bible application could solve anything. Of course, neither of them had a clue about the real world.

She would never argue with her father about his simplistic

beliefs, but Jarred was different. He might be Dust Bowl born and bred, but he was also a college graduate, for heaven's sake. He should know better than to embrace such a small town mentality. "Honestly Jarred, do you think that was written to be taken literally?" she challenged.

His eyes never left the road. "Absolutely."

She shook her head at his unwavering tone. It was obvious he wouldn't be moved on that point. "Okay, let's assume, for the sake of argument, it was intended to be taken as written. That portion of the Bible was written almost two thousand years ago. People back then couldn't possibly foresee the pressures and worries of the twentieth century."

"I agree."

Abigail was immediately suspicious. Jarred never gave in that easily. "You do?"

"Sure. No man could possibly foresee the future. But," he added with emphasis, "the Bible is not merely the writings of men. Paul's second letter to Timothy says it's the inspired word of God. And God knew without a doubt what was to come. As our loving Father, He gave us His Word, the Bible, as a blueprint for living successful, meaningful, peaceful lives in any century."

He smiled at the blatant skepticism he read in her face. "You don't have to take my word for it, Abby," he said as he reached over to gently squeeze her hand. "He wrote it down for you." He winked. "All you have to do is look."

Abigail fell silent. In spite of their obvious differences of opinion, she couldn't be angry with him. In fact, she actually envied Jarred's confidence in God. Not so long ago she shared it. But now she knew the truth. Neither God nor simple Bible passages had any place in the real-world formula for success.

She'd made it a point since college to study those people fortunate enough to be considered a success. While many pointed to their education, job, or well-placed connections, few, if any, attributed their attainment of social prominence and wealth to God.

That was not to say she didn't love or revere God anymore, because she did. And any Sunday when she wasn't busy, she'd be glad to go to church. Unfortunately, in the year she'd lived in the city the priority of making something of oneself left little time for spiritual interests.

Her gaze and thoughts turned toward the window where she watched the familiar landscape rush by. *Late spring is such a lovely time in Dust Bowl,* she mused. She didn't remember everything could be so green and alive. Locked away in the concrete confines of the city, she'd almost forgotten what pure sunshine looked like.

Jarred swung the truck off Main Street and headed north on the farm road bordering his ranch. Contented Herefords dotted the fields, grazing on the lush foliage of the wide open pasture.

"So where did you build the house?" Abigail asked as she scanned the horizon.

"Remember Blackberry Hill where we used to climb to pick blackberries?"

Abigail nodded. "How could I forget it?" she answered ruefully. "You and Phillip tied me up and left me stranded there for hours."

"That's only because you were spying on us," he defended with a laugh. "We were honor-bound to take you prisoner after you breached the security of our fort. Anyway, to answer your question, the house stands on the very top of the hill."

She turned to consider him. "You always said you'd build up there one day."

"You know me, Abby." He shrugged, favoring her with a cocky grin. "Once I set my mind on something there's no backing down."

He turned right onto an unpaved road leading up to Blackberry Hill. Great clouds of dust swirled behind the truck as it rumbled up the incline. When they reached the crest, he shifted the truck into park and pointed straight ahead. "There it is!" he pronounced proudly.

Abigail followed the line of his finger, squinting to see through the churning dust. As the dirt finally settled she could see clearly. She stared for a long moment before turning to Jarred.

"That's it?" she demanded incredulously.

"Well, yes," Jarred stammered, "I know it's not much. Yet."

"That has to be the understatement of the year." She pinned him with a furious stare. "Jarred, it's a foundation!"

eight

Abigail surveyed the concrete platform with dismay. "It's just a foundation," she repeated, shaking her head.

"I knew you'd pick up on that right away, being a sharp city girl and all."

She whirled on him, glaring into his smiling face. "Very funny," she snapped sarcastically. "Let me guess—this is another cute prank you and my brother cooked up."

Jarred was obviously taken aback by her reaction. "Now, Abby," he began, reaching out to take her hand.

She slapped his hand away. "Don't you 'now, Abby' me, Jarred Worth!" she growled through clenched teeth. She was seething. It was all a prank! She'd been worried sick for a solid week about making this trip, but she did it—drove here out of some misguided sense of friendship and loyalty to be the butt of a joke.

"Abby, honey, you've got to believe me," Jarred cajoled, "it's no joke." He pointed to the concrete form. "You're looking at my new place."

She cut her eyes at him.

"It's true," he insisted. "It's just in the early stages, that's all. I meant it when I said I need your input." His eyes held an apology as he added, "I guess I should have mentioned it would require a bit of imagination too. At least, for a while."

Abigail leaned her head back against the seat and closed her eyes. She absently pinched the bridge of her nose. *A little imagination,* she thought. *What an understatement.*

She started tearing the seals off of the new bottle of aspirin.

Jarred asked softly, "Headache, Abby?"

She refused to meet his eyes, choosing to continue her efforts to open the bottle. There was a definite chill in her voice when she answered, "I'm working on one."

"Here, let me see if I can help." Before she could protest he leaned across the seat and taking her by the shoulders he turned her toward the door, her back facing him.

"What are you—"

Abigail's protest fell silent as Jarred's long fingers massaged the base of her neck. She closed her eyes to savor the glorious sensation. After several minutes his strong hands fanned out to gently knead the tense muscles of her shoulders. She exhaled a long sigh of pure contentment.

"Better?" he whispered.

She thought she might melt. "Ummm."

"I guess you want me to take you home."

Abigail said nothing, her thoughts darting back to the conversation at her parents' breakfast table earlier that morning. "Abigail can make something from nothing," Jarred had said. And what was her mother's reply? She remembered thinking at the time it was an unusual response.

She concentrated harder. She could recall the bemused expression on her mother's face as they left to go "decorating." Suddenly, it all came back. Her mother had said, "That's a gift that'll come in mighty handy."

A giggle welled up inside her. The whole situation was so ridiculous. Her shoulders began to shake as mirth rumbled up her throat and erupted into laughter. "My gift…will come in…mighty handy," she chortled breathlessly between peals of laughter.

Jarred regarded her with a dubious expression. "What gift is that, Abby?"

"For making something from nothing!" She howled with glee.

Her laughter proved infectious and Jarred joined in. Seeing him laugh made Abigail laugh all the harder. They laughed for a full five minutes. When the hilarity was finally spent, Abigail wiped away the last tears of mirth with the back of her hand.

"Do you want—I mean, would you consider looking around?" The look in Jarred's dark eyes matched the hopeful tone of his deep voice.

"Why not?" Abigail answered with an amiable shrug, her good nature restored.

Abigail looped her arm through Jarred's and he escorted her across the swaying green grasses of the tree-shaded lot to stand beside the foundation. He motioned toward the air directly in front of them. "This is the front door."

"Lovely," Abigail said with a grin. "Shall we go in?"

She stepped up on the concrete when Jarred's strong hands

dropped onto her shoulders to restrain her.

"Wait."

In response to her look of bewilderment he explained, "I want to get the door for you." He swung open the imaginary door with a flourish. "I wouldn't want you to bump your head. I know how prone you are to headaches."

"Clown!" Abigail gave him a playful shove.

"To begin our tour," he said with a sweeping gesture to his right, "you'll find the formal dining room. I don't know if you noticed, but the entire downstairs has twelve-foot ceilings."

"Oh, I did," she quipped, gazing up into the cloudless blue Oklahoma sky. "I'm sure that's why it has such an airy feeling."

Jarred chuckled. "If you walk through here," he led the way farther across the foundation, "you'll find the kitchen."

Abigail looked around as though she could actually see something other than the few white PVC pipes protruding from the concrete floor. "Very spacious."

"I hoped you'd think so." He took her arm and directed her toward the left. "This is the living area. I planned for it to be one large room, not too formal. The fieldstone fireplace is there," he said, pointing across the floor, "and the room is framed in ten-foot windows."

Abigail regarded him with mock seriousness. "That must be what gives the place that wide-open feeling."

Jarred ruffled her hair. "The master bedroom is along the back of the house and my office is next to the living room. That completes the tour of the downstairs. You'll have to wait until I get the banister up to see the second floor," he said, pointing upwards into space. Other than the glimmer of mischief in his eyes, his expression was the picture of sincerity as he said, "We don't want to risk you falling on your sensitive head!"

She couldn't help but laugh.

On completion of their mock tour, Jarred and Abigail "stepped outside" to tour the lot. A steady breeze, fragrant with the newness of spring, buffeted the couple as they strolled side by side along the grassy hilltop.

"Oh, Jarred!" Abigail cried with delight, pointing toward a dark green patch of foliage. "You saved the blackberries!"

He grinned down at her. "You bet. Couple more weeks and they'll be ripe. I can almost taste your momma's blackberry cobbler." He smacked his lips in anticipation. "You remember all the fun we used to have pickin' berries, Abby?" Jarred's long fingers gently brushed back a strand of golden hair that had blown into her eyes. "You, me, and Phillip racing to see who could fill their pail first?"

"I remember you and Phillip eating the berries out of my bucket when I wasn't looking," she replied with forced indignance. "I never could figure out why you two always beat me."

Jarred studied her with a tender expression in his eyes. "Guess we gave you a pretty tough time, huh, kid?"

"The toughest," she agreed. "But," she admitted with an impish grin, "I loved every minute of it."

Jarred wrapped his arms around her, squeezing her in an affectionate hug. "You're pretty special, Abigail Bradley."

The casual embrace rendered Abigail breathless, the same tingly sensation she'd experienced at breakfast. What was going on? She knew the gesture meant nothing, simply a warm hug from a dear friend, but that knowledge did nothing to stem the shivery tide racing up her spine. To make matters worse, she was horrified to hear her own traitorous sigh of disappointment when he released her.

Jarred grinned down at her and his dimples, so often the source of her discomfort, reassured her nothing was amiss. They were friends. Period.

They spent the rest of morning and part of the afternoon wandering around the property laughing and reminiscing about the old times. The year's separation dropped away effortlessly, leaving the comfortable feeling that they'd never been apart.

"Guess I ought to be getting you home," Jarred said, reluctance coloring his deep voice.

"Yeah." Abigail's response was equally unenthusiastic.

The carefree mood of the day became noticeably somber as they made their way back to the truck. Neither spoke as Jarred drove down the hill and back through the center of town.

Main Street was bustling with its customary Saturday afternoon activity. Abigail watched as a steady stream of traffic filtered through the front door of the drugstore. In addition to a widely varied inventory from ant traps to zippers, it boasted a soda fountain second to none. She smiled at the many happy memories she held from that place.

As they stopped for the red light, Dust Bowl's sole traffic signal, Abigail admired the storefront windows glistening in the warm afternoon sun. Despite her efforts to cultivate disdain for her rural roots, she still loved the old places. The sophisticated high rises of the big city would never match the beauty of these aging brick structures. There was a comforting sense of permanence here. And a sense of home.

Jarred turned off onto her parents' narrow, tree-lined street and pulled up into their driveway. She waited as he hopped out of the truck and came around to open the door for her. "I've been thinking," he said as he swung open the door, "that maybe, if you don't have any other plans, you'll have dinner with me tonight out at my place." His gaze flickered toward her before resting on some faraway sight. "As a way to say thanks for coming home to help me this weekend."

Abigail jumped at the opportunity to extend such a wonderful day. "I'd love to," she answered without hesitation.

"Great! I'll pick you up at six," he called to her as she headed up the walk. She waved her acknowledgment before ducking into the house.

≈

A short three hours later Abigail was once again seated in Jarred's dusty pickup. He parked in one of the diagonal spaces along Main Street and disappeared into Audrey's Eats. Several minutes later he reappeared with a huge wicker hamper in tow.

"What's all that?" she asked as he climbed in beside her.

"Dinner, and if it tastes half as good as it smells, we're going to have a feast."

He swung the pickup out into the light stream of traffic. It took Abigail a minute to realize where they were headed.

"Why are we going back toward Blackberry Hill?"

He looked surprised. "I thought I mentioned we'd be eating at my place."

"Well, yes, you did," Abigail said slowly. "But I thought you meant your parents' house." She knew Jarred had been living in the small house at the corner of his ranch that had belonged to his parents before they passed away.

He shook his head. "Lacks atmosphere."

Abigail grinned. "I've got to admit that's the one thing your new place has plenty of. Atmosphere, I mean."

They were still chuckling companionably as Jarred pulled the truck to a halt at the top of the hill. The sun was low now, and the cool evening air was already settling around them. Abigail pulled her cotton sweater around her shoulders more tightly.

Her doubts as to the suitability of a cold concrete floor for a picnic were quickly assuaged when Jarred began to set up for dinner. She stood back, watching as first he pulled two propane lanterns from the back of his truck and set them in the "dining room." Next, he lifted a tarp and an old quilt from the back and spread them on the foundation for a table. Finally, he carried the hamper out and rested it in the middle of the quilt.

"Supper's on," he called.

Abigail was astonished by the amount of food he extracted from the basket. Smoked ribs, barbecued beans, potato salad, cole slaw, dill pickles, and a plastic container filled with iced tea. All that and an entire pecan pie for dessert.

After Jarred asked the blessing, they filled their plates and settled down to some serious eating when Jarred sprang to his feet. "Oops, I forgot something."

He jogged back to the truck and returned with two candles. "Don't want to forget these," he said with a wink, lighting them and arranging the globes at the upper corners of the quilt.

The candles caught Abigail off guard. "Jarred, I had no idea you were such a romantic," she said before she could stop the words from tumbling out of her mouth.

Jarred choked on his iced tea. "Romantic?" he sputtered between coughs. "Didn't know you were looking for romance, Abby. Afraid these won't count. They're citronella candles."

Citronella? The candles were to ward off mosquitoes! "Oh, I knew that," Abigail claimed with a self-conscious laugh. "It was just a joke. I mean, romance between friends? Ridiculous." *What is the matter with me today?* Nobody knew better than she that they were just friends. She determined not to forget again.

Dinner was finished, the plates and plastic utensils disposed of, and the leftovers tucked away in the hamper when Jarred and Abigail sat back, side by side, to watch the sun disappear beneath a luxuriously painted sky. They studied the spectacular display in awed silence while crickets on the hillside chirped an accompaniment.

Little by little tiny stars appeared, dotting the darkened sky. A delicious sense of quiet washed over Abigail as she sat next to Jarred, staring up into the glittering heavens. She sighed deeply.

He reached over to squeeze her hand. "My sentiments exactly."

"You were right to build here, Jarred," she whispered. "It's perfect."

"Perfect," he repeated as he draped his arm around her shoulders, the movement bringing his face within inches of hers. Their eyes met under the starlit sky. His voice was a husky whisper as he said, "The only thing that would make this more perfect—"

Suddenly his eyes widened. Jarred stiffened and dropped his arm as though he'd been burned. "The only thing that would make this more perfect," his second try sounded more like a croak. He cleared his throat. "Would be if you'd look at the blueprints." He sprang to his feet. "Want to see them?"

Abigail was bewildered by his strange behavior. She'd never known Jarred to be jumpy. Perhaps she'd really spooked him with that comment about romance. Poor soul. He was behaving as weird as she felt.

She decided to act as if nothing were out of the ordinary. "I'd love to see them."

After retrieving them from the truck, Jarred unrolled the huge sheets of paper, pressed them flat against the quilt, and tucked the upper corners under the now lit propane lanterns. Abigail flopped down on her stomach and propped her face in her hands to study the drawings in the flickering light.

Jarred joined her on the quilt and for an hour or so they studied the blueprints, with Abigail offering her approval or an occasional suggestion for minor modifications.

Several times her attention wandered as his shoulder accidentally brushed against hers. As a gust of breeze carried his familiar scent to her, her thoughts filtered back to the night of graduation when he'd held her for those brief moments.

Jarred rolled onto his back. He folded his hands behind his head and stared up into the starry sky. "Guess we'd better be getting back. Church is at nine tomorrow."

"I'm afraid I won't be able to make it to church." Abigail kept her eyes trained on the blueprints to avoid lying directly to his face. "I've got to get back to the city."

That was partially true, she assured her reproving conscience. She'd fulfilled her promise to Jarred and now it was time to get back. It was also true that she had plenty of time to attend church in the morning. But she wouldn't. She just couldn't face all the people.

They packed up the truck and rode home in comfortable silence.

"Tell me honestly," Jarred said, leaning his arm on the wall behind her as they stood at the door of her parents' house. "What did you think of the house—uh, the plans?" he amended with a boyish grin.

"It's beautiful," she admitted. "A real dream house." A tiny frown marred her face as she raised her eyes to his. "Something puzzles me though."

"Yes?"

"Why in the world do you need so much space? The house is over three thousand square feet."

Jarred flashed her his signature grin, complete with arresting dimples. "Aw, Abby, that's easy." He ruffled her hair playfully. "It's not just for me."

"It's not?"

"Nope. I'm planning to get married."

nine

"Married?" Lurline's high pitched squeal could easily be heard for two city blocks.

"That's what he said."

Lurline downed the entire contents of her cup in a gulp and deposited it on Abigail's desk with a thump. "You better tell me the whole story again. This time, real slow."

"We'd just gotten back to my parents' house after a picnic dinner out at the site where he's building his new house. I could tell from the blueprints it's going to be enormous, and I asked him why he needed so much space. He said he was planning to get married."

"Just like that?" Lurline leaned forward to cross examine her friend. "Didn't you ask him any details?"

Abigail lifted her slight shoulders in a shrug. "The news came as such a surprise, I couldn't say anything. Not that it would have mattered. As soon as he made the announcement, he practically sprinted out to his truck and raced away in a cloud of dust."

Lurline slumped back into her chair. "I gotta tell ya, this comes as a big surprise to me. I know you kept saying you two were just friends and all, but I truly thought there was more to it."

She offered an apologetic grimace to Abigail. "Maybe it was the goose bumps on your arms, or maybe it was the weird way your face lights up when you talk about Jarred, but I figured—" She paused to look closely into her friend's face. "This is okay, isn't it? I mean, you're not upset or anything about him getting married, are you?"

"It's for the best, Lurline."

Lurline's relief was obvious. "I'm really glad to hear you say that. For a minute there, I was afraid you might have some regrets."

Abigail shook her head. "No regrets," she said, staring down at her hands. "I admit going home this weekend stirred up some pretty strange feelings for me. Feelings for Dust Bowl and Ja—" She stopped and raised her eyes to Lurline's. "I realize now that

I needed something concrete to close that chapter of my past. Jarred's news has helped me do that.

"I'd be lying if I didn't say that Dust Bowl is a great place." A smile softened the corners of her mouth. "The country is so beautiful—the air seems cleaner there, the sky seems bluer—" She laughed. "It even smells better in Dust Bowl. I can't explain it—" her voice faded away into thoughtful silence.

New purpose shone in Abigail's eyes. "You and I both know that a rural background is nothing but a hindrance to making something of ourselves. It's time to move on. A year ago we set our sights on success and I see no reason to change plans now."

Lurline clapped her on the back. "We're gonna be successful, I just know it. Why, look at you. Since you met Edward at the *Herald's* charity bazaar, you've been to some really classy places. You've been meeting the people we've be reading about in the society pages. If that ain't making something of yourself, I don't know what is."

Abigail smiled at her ever-loyal friend. "It's a beginning."

ঽ

Jarred guided his pickup up to the rusted gas pump and switched off the engine. Before he could climb out of the truck, Phillip Bradley appeared at his window.

"Mornin', Jarred. Fill it up for you?"

"I'd appreciate it."

Phillip got the pump started and reappeared, frowning at Jarred through the window. "Glad you came by this morning," he said, leaning on the door frame. "I wanted to talk to you."

Jarred eyed his friend quizzically. It was unlike Phillip to be so serious. "Shoot."

"It's about my sister—"

Raw fear shot up Jarred's spine. "Abby?" His voice raised in alarm. "What's the matter? Has something happened to her?"

Phillip smiled for the first time that morning. "Far as I know," he drawled with maddening calm, "she's back in the city and doing just fine."

Jarred relaxed. "For heaven's sake!" He glared ferociously at the other man. "Don't scare me like that!"

"Might jumpy there, pal," Phillip teased. "My little sister

upsetting you?"

"I'm not jumpy," Jarred denied, his heart rate slowing to normal.

Phillip folded his arms across his chest and remarked casually, "I was surprised to see Abby at home over the weekend. It's been over a year since she's spent that much time here." He leaned down to stare into Jarred's face. "You wouldn't know anything about her mysterious appearance, would you?"

Jarred met his eyes steadily. "I asked her to come home, if that's what you're fishing for."

"Just like that? You asked her and she makes a beeline for home?" Phillip scratched his jaw. "Isn't that incredible?" he said, the skepticism in his voice mirroring his disbelief. "You figure all this time she was just waiting for someone to issue a formal invitation?" He shook his head. "Must be big city etiquette."

Jarred gave an amused snort. "I can see you're not going to be satisfied until you get the full scoop."

"You know me too well," Phillip confessed with a grin. He swung Jarred's door open. "Come on in. I'll buy you a cup of coffee and you can tell me all about it."

Jarred followed Phillip into the tiny office of the station where the coffee maker stood on a table in the corner. Phillip filled two cracked ceramic cups from the steaming pot and handed one to Jarred, who accepted his with a smile of thanks.

Jarred drank deeply of the aromatic brew before resting the cup on the counter by the antiquated cash register. "Not much to tell," he said. "I asked Abby to come. I ran into her at the stock show and told her I needed some help decorating my new place. You know how she loves fixing things up."

"What are you talking about, your new place? You don't have a new place."

"Sure I do." Jarred grinned broadly. "Or rather, I will. Poured the foundation about a week ago. Up on Blackberry Hill."

Phillip was silent for a moment. "Let me get this straight. You saw my sister at the stock show, a little less than two weeks ago, right?"

Jarred nodded.

"You invited her to come help you decorate a house that you

didn't start building until a week later?" Phillip pinned him with a reproachful look. "One that you hadn't even *mentioned* to your best friend." He lowered his cup. "You've obviously got something up your sleeve."

"Sounds pretty incriminating, doesn't it?" Jarred agreed, rubbing his jaw thoughtfully.

"Aren't you even going to deny it?"

Jarred shook his head. "Can't."

Phillip sighed in exasperation. "Then would you mind explaining it to your old buddy?"

Jarred picked up his cup and gazed into the steamy liquid. "That's easy," he said without looking up. "I'm in love with Abby."

"You're in love with my little sister?" Phillip repeated in a voice an octave higher than normal. "With *Abby?*"

Jarred grinned into the incredulous face of his long-time friend. "You, of all people, should know how I feel about Abby. I've been telling you for years."

"Well sure—but I didn't know you meant it like that."

"Phillip, I've been in love with your little sister since I was a kid." Jarred stared past him through the plate glass window. "I can still remember seeing her for the very first time." A smile lit his face as the image focused in his mind. "I had stopped by your house after school and there she was, lying on the couch, all wrapped up in a white blanket.

"Huh?"

Jarred turned to watch the light of understanding dawn slowly in his friend's eyes.

"You're talking about the day my mom brought her home from the hospital!" Phillip cried in disbelief. "That's crazy! You couldn't possibly have been in love with her then. For crying out loud, she was a baby. You were only six years old!"

Jarred shrugged. "Beats all, doesn't it? All I know is that I took one look into her perfect little face and she stole my heart. I can't explain it exactly, but it was like even as a kid, I knew she was a part of me."

Phillip dropped into the battered chair behind the cash register. "Wow." He looked up to consider his best friend. "Does that mean you were serious when you offered my mom your pet raccoon in exchange for Abby?"

Jarred chuckled. "Very serious. I was crushed when she turned me down. I'd already gone home and cleaned out my sock drawer to keep Abby in." He shook his head at the memory. "Let me assure you, the feelings I have for Abby now are slightly different from back then."

Phillip raked his hands through his sandy blond hair. "Okay, we've established the staggering fact that you are truly in love with Abby. Are you telling me you're crazy enough to build a house just to get her to come home for a visit?"

"I've been planning to build a place up on that hill for a long time, Phillip. It's just when I ran into Abby at the stock show I realized I needed to step up the timetable a bit, that's all."

"You've lost me again, pal."

"Since your momma wisely turned down my offer for a trade, I've been waiting for Abby to get to the age when she could speak for herself." Jarred studied the scuffed toes of his boots. "I hoped that after she graduated from college, I could talk her into marrying me." He flashed Phillip a wry grin. "Unfortunately, things didn't work out the way I planned."

Phillip scowled. "Sending Abby away to school was a mistake. That fancy college filled her head with all kinds of foolishness. Like Dust Bowl's not good enough."

"Be easy on her, pal. Remember what it was like when we went to college, country boy?"

"Yeah," Phillip agreed. "We sure got razzed." He looked hopefully at his friend. "You think that's what's got into Abby? Like that big fuss she made at the church supper when she was shouting about being somebody?"

Jarred nodded. "I s'pect it is. Somehow she's gotten confused about things." He sipped his coffee thoughtfully. "I can't say it's a bad thing." The sharp look Phillip shot him told him he needed to clarify his position. "She needs to think for herself. She's got to come to a decision as to whether the things she's been raised to believe are true."

Phillip shook his head. "You *must* be in love with her."

Jarred's dark brow shot up with question.

"Only someone blinded by love could find any good in the

way Abby's been acting. Personally, I think she's an idiot, turning her back on the people she loves. But it's her decision to
make. After all, she's an adult."

"I noticed that right off," Jarred said with a grin. "Our little
Abby is all grown up." He frowned slightly. "Unfortunately, we're
not the only ones to notice. There's at least one city fella hot on
her trail."

He drained the contents of his cup before saying, "That's why
I needed to get moving on the house. I need a good excuse to get
her to come back home and spend some time with her—before I
spring my feelings on her."

"Why wait? I know she thinks the world of you." A wide grin
spread across Phillip's face as he voiced a new thought, "Who
knows, maybe she's been in love with you, too, and she's just
waiting to hear it from you first."

"Don't I wish." Jarred gave a self-deprecating laugh. "Truth is,
I've messed up things pretty bad. I opened my big mouth on
Saturday night and before I knew what happened, I told her I was
planning to get married."

Jarred swept his hat from his head, and ran his fingers
through his hair. "It was the oddest thing," he said, mostly to
himself. "I sure hadn't planned to say anything, but I got to
looking into those big blue eyes of hers and I forgot everything. Mind went blank." He shook his head in dismay.
"Doesn't seem right for a woman to have that effect on a
man. It's downright embarrassing."

Phillip's eyes looked suspiciously bright and he held a fist
over his mouth as he snickered, "What'd you do?"

"What do you think? I lit out quick, before I could say anything else."

Phillip exploded into laughter.

Jarred fixed him with a dark stare. "I'm glad someone finds this
amusing."

"I'm sorry, Jarred, it's just that you look so—so pitiful." He
sobered slightly at the scowl on his friend's face. "Never mind
. What happened?"

Nothing." Jarred's tone of voice and expression reflected his
ry. "She headed back to the city first thing Sunday morning,

and I've been kicking myself over handling things so badly."

Both men fell silent. A bell jangled and Phillip went outside to gas up Cal Brunson's dilapidated truck. Minutes later Phillip stepped back into the station wiping his hands on a rag. "So what are you going to do about my sister?" His concern was evident by the expression on his face. "You're not going to give up on her, are you?"

Jarred scooped his hat off the counter and plopped it onto his head. "Never."

Phillip relaxed visibly. "Good. So what can I do?"

Jarred strode to the doorway and paused to look back at Phillip before stepping out into the early morning light. "You can do the same thing I've been doing every day for the last twenty-two years."

"And that is?"

"Pray."

ten

The determination to put Dust Bowl and Jarred Worth behind drove Abigail to new heights of productivity. She told Lurline nothing had changed and she meant it. Dust Bowl was now relegated to the past, the unsuccessful past. She'd committed to making something of herself and she was going to do it.

What she hadn't told Lurline was just how deeply Jarred's announcement had affected her. A dull ache had taken up residence in her heart.

She remembered hearing somewhere there was no better remedy for melancholy than good old-fashioned hard work, so she attacked the Notebook submissions with a vengeance. By lunch time Thursday, Abigail had one final submission to enter—a full five hours before deadline.

She picked up the last piece of paper from the stack and began to type. *Local weight loss group will hold its monthly meeting at the Cedar Hill Ice Cream Delights, Tuesday 6 P.M. The topic will be "Meeting and Beating Temptation—Facing Down the Enemy." Refreshments to follow.*

"You busy?"

Abigail glanced up from her typing to see Suzanne Masters smiling brightly.

"Very." Abigail returned her attention to her computer screen with the hope Suzanne would get the message and go away.

"I thought you might like to have lunch."

Abigail's fingers froze on the keyboard. Her incredulous gaze climbed slowly to meet Suzanne's. "Me?"

Suzanne nodded.

"Let me get this straight. *You* want to have lunch with *me?*"

Suzanne seemed unperturbed by the question. "Sure. I thought we'd try out that new French restaurant on Sixth Avenue."

Abigail cocked a finely arched brow as she searched for some indication Suzanne was joking. In the entire year Abigail had been with the *Herald,* Suzanne's only contact had been to needle her.

"Well?" Suzanne asked after a long moment of silence. "My treat."

Abigail's eyes widened slightly. Suzanne was serious. Something was definitely going on.

Despite nearly overwhelming curiosity about the strange invitation, Abigail's initial reaction was to decline the offer. It was a matter of principle. Suzanne Masters was an overbearing snob whose chief aim was to make her life miserable.

"I'm sorry, Suzanne—"

She stopped as she suddenly remembered Lurline had a dentist appointment and wouldn't be back until mid-afternoon. That changed things a bit. Having lunch with anybody, even a snob, beat eating a cold meatloaf sandwich alone. It didn't hurt that the snob was treating.

"What I meant to say is, yes, I'd love to."

❧

"Bon jour, ladies." The maitre d' bowed slightly. "I have zee perfect place for you. Follow me." The perfect place was a small round lace-covered table waiting in the very center of the room.

"Couldn't we find somewhere a little less conspicuous?" Abigail whispered after a quick glance around the room. "I feel like I'm in a fishbowl."

"Nonsense," Suzanne said with a dismissive little wave. "What's the point of going to the right places if you aren't going to be seen?" She accepted the proffered seat from the maitre d' with royal aplomb and signaled for Abigail to join her.

"If you're worried your dress isn't suitable," Suzanne continued, regarding Abigail's clothing with a disdainful grimace, "then I suggest you revamp your wardrobe. A word to the wise. Real women don't do polyester. And another thing. As my mother always said, 'It's a wise woman who remembers she is on display and dresses accordingly.' "

Abigail sat down in a self-conscious hurry. "Did your mother really say that?" She was genuinely intrigued over the fundamental differences in their backgrounds. *The only thing my mother ever told me was to be sure to wear underwear without holes.*

Suzanne nodded.

Abigail resolved to take her wardrobe a bit more seriously. Of course, it would be a whole lot easier to be serious if her clothing budget wasn't such a joke.

An interesting thought about successful people came to light as Abigail unfolded the napkin in her lap. First, Suzanne admitted she selected restaurants on the basis of being seen. Secondly, she said she chose her wardrobe for display. This concept of doing things entirely for show was a new one for Abigail, the antithesis of everything she'd been taught at home. Somehow, it didn't seem right.

She smiled and accepted the menu from the hovering waiter, ignoring her untimely twinge of conscience. Right or not, it was the way of successful people. And who was she, Abigail from Dust Bowl, to argue with an authority?

Abigail's eyes widened with the awesome revelation that Suzanne was truly an authority on success. Sure, she'd been born into money and position, but even so, she had taken it a step farther—she was the society reporter for one of the largest newspapers in the state.

Perhaps I've been going about this Suzanne thing all wrong, Abigail thought as she hoisted her menu high to afford herself a meager bit of privacy. Instead of seeing Suzanne as the enemy, forever separated from Abigail by the wide chasm of success, it would be better to see her as a role model, a person to imitate.

"Isn't that Deidre Harrington over there?" Suzanne whispered from the other side of the laminated barrier.

Abigail lowered her menu to check.

"For heaven's sake," Suzanne gasped. "Don't look at her!"

Abigail snapped the menu back in place.

"I must say," Suzanne continued in a calmer tone, "I'm surprised to see her up so early."

Abigail chanced lowering the menu slightly. "Why?"

"You haven't heard?" Suzanne's eyes were wide with disbelief. Seeing that Abigail hadn't, she explained importantly, "The Kirbys had a little soiree last night. Everybody was there. The party was still going strong when I left, about two A.M." Suzanne lowered her voice to confide, "It seems Deidre capped off the evening by taking a dip in the Kirby's pool. Fully dressed! You can always count on Deidre to liven things up."

Abigail stole a peek at the elegant woman in question. Edward had introduced them at the ballet and Abigail remembered thinking how happy the woman was, a perpetual smile on her face. She sighed wistfully. Why shouldn't Deidre be happy? Here was a woman who had it all: money, fabulous clothes, and a place in high society.

"Oh, look!" Suzanne cried after the waiter had taken their order. "There's Mary Alice Munson."

Abigail glanced carefully in the direction Suzanne indicated.

"She told me she's redecorating her entire home for a layout in *Beautiful Homes* magazine. Edwardo Vancinti has agreed to do the job." Suzanne pronounced his name with a dreamy sort of reverence.

Abigail drew a blank. "Edwardo Vancinti?"

Suzanne rolled her eyes heavenward. "Don't you know anything, Abigail? Edwardo Vancinti just happens to be the decorating genius of all time. She's flying him down from New York." She leaned over the table to whisper, "I understand his services go for in excess of one thousand dollars a day."

Suzanne proved to be a gold mine of information. By the time the women had finished their lunch and the waiter delivered the check, she had provided Abigail with running commentary of everyone in the room.

Abigail was awestruck. "How is it you know so much about everyone?"

"I am the society page reporter," Suzanne replied matter-of-factly. "It's my business to know."

"Don't they mind you divulging their secrets to the public?"

Suzanne chuckled. "Abigail, you are so funny. No, of course they don't mind. They love it. I give their lives meaning." She saw the look of confusion on Abigail's face and went on to clarify, "When I feature them in my column, I make their lives sound idyllic, fulfilled. I tell the public what it wants to hear; that the life of the privileged is one big fairy tale."

Abigail nodded solemnly. "And it is, isn't it?"

Suzanne's burst of laughter was genuine. "You are a riot," she managed between chortles. "I never appreciated what a sense of humor you have. Anyway," she said after regaining her composure, "I've invited you to lunch today because the public will want to read about you."

"Me?" Abigail stammered.

"Don't look so surprised. Edward Winters is a very prominent citizen and you two have been seeing quite a bit of each other."

"Well," Abigail admitted, "we've gotten together a few times."

"The ballet, dinner at Hubert's, and several appearances at the club are more than getting together a few times."

Abigail's eyes flew open. "How'd you—"

"I'd like," Suzanne interrupted impatiently, "permission to mention you two in my column—nothing too detailed you understand—just where I've seen you, what you were wearing, that sort of thing."

"You want to write about me?" Abigail repeated while her mind conjured up images of her picture splashed across the society page. This was beyond her wildest dreams. She schooled her expression to one of what she hoped was sophisticated nonchalance and said, "That would be lovely, Suzanne." She gave a casual flick of her wrist indicating the outcome made no matter to her either way. "Provided, of course, something comes up."

Underneath the table, the fingers on Abigail's other hand were tightly crossed.

eleven

Heavy clouds obscured the sun and cast the normally shady downtown area in a particularly dismal light. As Abigail drove along the crowded streets she wondered if she'd ever banish the longing she felt for the wide open country of Dust Bowl.

It was a little before ten when she swung her car into the parking place in front of Lurline's apartment and tooted the horn. Almost immediately, the door swung open and her statuesque friend appeared with a wide grin on her face and a stack of magazines in her arms. She locked the door of her apartment with some difficulty and strode out to the car.

"I brought along some reference materials," she said, dumping the load of magazines on the floor of the car and climbing in.

"Good morning to you, too." Abigail eyed the mountain at Lurline's feet. "I thought we were going shopping."

"No," Lurline corrected. "Power shopping."

Abigail pulled out of the parking lot and merged into the already heavy traffic. "I take it there's a difference."

"You bet there is. I read about it in this magazine." Lurline bent over and picked up a copy of *Fashion Forever*. She opened it to a page she had marked and read aloud, "'Power shopping is defining your mission, mobilizing your resources, plotting your game plan, and attacking with purpose.'"

Abigail frowned. "Sounds like war."

"Not at all. It's a systematic approach to fashion acquisition. According to this article, it's the wave of the future."

"I'll have to take your word for it." Abigail switched her attention to navigating an unusually congested intersection. Once safely on the other side she snapped her hand to her forehead in a smart salute. "So, General, what's the plan?"

"I'm glad you asked. I took the liberty of sketching out a mission statement last night." Lurline withdrew a crumpled piece of paper from the pocket of her jeans. "We're going to remake you."

"I don't think I can afford it."

"You have no choice," Lurline proclaimed solemnly. "Your wardrobe must say success. I read in *Extravagance* magazine

that your clothing makes a statement about you before you open
your mouth to speak."

Both pairs of eyes lowered self-consciously to examine their
own attire.

Abigail grimaced. "I think my outfit needs to have its mouth
washed out with soap!"

Lurline nodded in agreement. "Never mind. Help is on the way."

In minutes, Abigail pulled into the multilevel parking lot of the
mall. Lurline was out of the car in an instant. "Attack!"

Inside, the downtown mall was a three-level structure of glass
and steel. An open atrium in the center with lush foliage and
burbling waterfalls gave the impression of a tropical island instead of a shopping center.

"Let's start in here." Lurline tugged her friend toward a small
boutique. "Chez Elite. I've seen this place written up in all the
magazines. They cater to the society crowd. Classy stuff."

"I don't know, Lurline," Abigail said, hanging back. "It looks
awfully. . .exclusive, don't you think?"

Lurline patted her arm reassuringly. "It'll be fine. Just let me
handle the talking."

Inside the boutique, a reed thin clerk robed in stark black studied the twosome with undisguised disdain. "May I help you?"

Lurline was not deterred. "My friend has recently come into
some money and would like to spend it." When her statement
gained no reaction from the haughty woman, Lurline prompted,
"On clothes."

The clerk who had positioned herself between the women and
the shop held her ground. "What kind of clothing did you have
in mind?" she queried imperiously.

Lurline raised her pointed chin a fraction. "Something upwardly
mobile. With pizzazz."

Abigail could see the clerk struggling to suppress her amusement. Nonetheless, she acquiesced and stepped back, allowing
them access to the shop. "Perhaps you'd like to look around."

"You bet we would," Lurline agreed, still oblivious to the clerk's
animosity. Once out of earshot of the clerk she confided, "You've
just got to know how to handle these city types. The key here is
finesse."

In her best imitation of finesse, Abigail crossed over to the first rounder of clothes and started to flip through the dresses. Lurline's sources were right. The clothes were lovely.

She stopped to finger the cool silks and rough linens. She could easily imagine Suzanne wearing any one of these fine garments. Something about the cut of the dresses or drape of the fabric spoke of good taste.

"My word!" Lurline screeched from several rounders away. "Would you look at this!" She held up a dress. "Do you know they're asking two hundred fifty dollars for this thing?"

Finesse forgotten, Abigail checked the tag on the houndstooth check suit she'd been admiring. *Four ninety-five!* She pulled her hand away as if the suit burned her. "Lurline," she whispered loudly, "let's get out of here."

They slunk past the sneering clerk and reentered the mall in a hurry. "Boy, howdy! How do they get away with prices like that?" Lurline ran a hand through her orange curls. "Not to worry though. There's plenty of other stores here. I'm sure they're much more reasonable."

                                  ஐ

Three hours later the twosome had retreated to a small table in the food court. Abigail slipped off a shoe and rubbed her heel. "My feet hurt. I'm exhausted. I want to go home."

"We can't. We haven't bought anything yet."

"I bought this corndog."

Lurline shook her head. "Food doesn't count. I'm talking fashion."

"I've got to tell you," Abigail said, wagging her corndog at her friend, "I'm sick of talking fashion. That's all we've done since we arrived. Frankly, my head is spinning from all the contradictory advice we've gotten this morning—and the prices."

She took a bite of her corndog. "It's hopeless, Lurline," she said around the mouthful. "Even if we knew what we were looking for, we couldn't afford it. I'm beginning to question whether this upwardly mobile thing is all it's cracked up to be."

Lurline recoiled in horror. "Don't say that! Everything we want is riding on this. You can't make something of yourself without the proper clothing, and if you don't make something of yourself, you'll never be truly happy."

She began flipping through the pages of a magazine she'd stuffed into her purse. "I admit, we've made a slow start, but we cannot abandon our mission because of a few setbacks. I think we may have made a slight tactical error in not narrowing the field." She stopped to point to a two-page layout. "Here's our answer.

"This says, 'Today's woman needs to establish an image for herself. The important thing is not the quantity of clothes a woman has, but the image they create. Avoid expensive trends and gravitate toward the classics. A few trademark pieces can go a long way.'" She looked up from the article to smile encouragingly at Abigail. "This sounds economical. All we need is a trademark look. What's your favorite color?"

Abigail shrugged. "Blue."

"Perfect. Blue can be your trademark. We just need to find a couple of nice pieces in blue, like slacks and skirts and jackets, that can be interchanged with each other. You'll have a complete wardrobe that says style in no time."

"I guess it could work."

"Of course it will work." Lurline pushed her chair out and bounded to her feet. "Let's go get 'em."

❧

"I had no idea there were so many shades of blue," Lurline muttered as they exited from the department store.

"Or how much wearing all that blue would make me look like a recruit for a military academy."

"Don't give up. Maybe it was just an unfortunate choice of color." Lurline stepped back to study her friend. "How do you feel about red?"

Abigail glared.

Lurline raised her hands in surrender. "You're right. Red's no good. Forget I even mentioned it."

"I say we forget the whole color theme concept."

"Fine. We're flexible." Lurline withdrew a second magazine from her purse as they were walking and searched the pages for inspiration. "Here we go!" She thumped the page gleefully. "Here's your trademark look. Hats."

She caught Abigail's pained expression. "I'm serious," Lurline insisted. "We're trying to make a statement here. What do hats say?"

"Hats say cold heads."

"Hats say confidence."

"No hats," Abigail said flatly.

Undaunted, Lurline flipped the pages faster. "I'm sure there's something in here—wait! I've got it!" she shouted, stopping dead in her tracks.

Fellow shoppers gave a wide berth to the twosome, obviously not wanting to risk exposure.

"What have you got?" Abigail asked impatiently.

"The answer to our problem. Trendy fashion statement, one-time expense, major impact." She wrinkled her brow. "Of course, placement is everything—"

"What exactly are we talking about here?"

"A tattoo."

"That does it." Abigail took off, her long strides practically a sprint.

"Wait!" Lurline ran to catch up. "Where are we going?"

"I don't know, but I'll know it when I see it."

"Abigail, you've got to work with me on this," Lurline pleaded breathlessly. "It says right here in *Fashion Forever*," she shook the magazine at Abigail for emphasis, "that your clothes have got to say: smart, stylish, successful—"

Abigail stopped suddenly. "That's it!"

Lurline skidded to a halt beside her. "I'm glad to have a little cooperation here. Now, as I was saying—"

"No. I mean that dress in the window. That's it."

"What dress? The ivory one? It's awfully plain."

"That's the one." Abigail ducked into the department store with Lurline dogging her heels.

"I don't know, Abigail, not much pizzazz. Tell me this; just what does that dress say?"

Abigail never slowed her pace. "Simplicity."

Lurline followed Abigail into the elevator. "Simplicity? I don't know—" She frantically scanned the pages of her last magazine. Suddenly a huge smile blossomed across her freckled face.

Abigail eyed her suspiciously. "Now what?"

"I think you just hit on something big. This article advocates replacing our closets full of fussy clothes with pieces chosen for their simplicity. They've got some guy named Thoreau quoted in here as saying, 'Simplify, simplify'."

❧

Suzanne hurried past Abigail's cubicle, her high heels clicking staccato on the tile floor. Suddenly, the clicking slowed and Suzanne's face appeared around the wall. "What's that you're wearing?" she demanded.

Abigail glanced down. "It's a dress."

"I can see that," she snapped impatiently. "Where did you get it?"

"At the mall." Abigail glanced down again, searching the new garment for a tear or stain. "Is something wrong?"

"It looks nice." It was obvious the statement wasn't made easily. "Really nice."

"Why, thank you." Suzanne's grudging praise made the nine grueling hours at the mall seem worthwhile. A spark of mischief ignited in her eyes and she couldn't resist repeating some of the fashion rhetoric Lurline had been preaching. "I've always felt it's so important that our clothes make the right statement."

Suzanne's eyes widened. "I had no idea you were interested in fashion."

"Absolutely," Abigail said solemnly. "I practically learned my alphabet in *Fashion First*." That was putting it on a bit thick. She had to chew the insides of her mouth to keep from laughing out loud. "I've never been one to embrace the latest trends, however. For myself, I prefer to rely on a few well chosen pieces for the mainstay of my wardrobe. How did Thoreau put it? 'Simplify, simplify'?"

❧

TIDBITS FROM SUZANNE

This reporter recently spotted Edward Winters and Abigail Bradley enjoying refreshments at the club. From my vantage point, things looked very cozy between this interesting couple. Ms. Bradley was wearing a simple dress of ivory linen, and I found myself admiring her sense of minimalist style in an age of overdone.

twelve

It was time for action.

Abigail's appearance with Edward Winters on the society page, the third appearance with him in the last three weeks, was proof positive that Jarred needed to do something. He dug his hands in his pockets as he paced across the building site on Blackberry Hill. But what?

He'd had plenty of advice. Since the paper arrived that morning, his phone rang off the wall with helpful suggestions from neighbors and friends. The Strade twins wanted Jarred to hire a detective to kidnap Abby and drag her back to Dust Bowl where she belonged. Phillip thought Jarred should drive into the city and declare his love for Abby. Immediately. Pastor Johnson recommended fasting and prayer. Abby's parents were the only ones without a specific plan of action, but it was their call that moved him the most.

"Jarred," her father had said, "we love you like a son. Been planning on having you for a son-in-law someday. I know you've been waiting for nature to take its course with Abby, and up until now, I've agreed with you. But these pictures of Abby and the city boy have me worried. You've got to do something."

Her father was right. It was time for action. He stopped to drive the toe of his boot into a massive clump of weeds. "What can I do?" He kicked at the cluster of leaves again and again. For a guy who always had the answers, Jarred suddenly found himself at a loss without one. And he didn't like it.

Despite his high hopes, Abby's visit three weeks ago was a disaster. For months, he'd been praying fervently for an opportunity to be with her. The fact that she came home was nothing short of a miracle. He knew he was given a chance to reestablish the bond of friendship they'd shared from childhood and then slowly build on it toward a love relationship that would last a lifetime.

The friendship part was easy. The years of separation by college and Abby's move to the city seemed to slip away, leaving the two friends as close as ever.

It was the part about gradually building onto the friendship that didn't go as planned. He rolled his eyes heavenward. What an understatement.

He'd been the picture of self-control with Abby on Saturday until her joking reference to romance over dinner that night. Then he'd lost it.

Jarred believed himself to be an intelligent man, rational and articulate, but one look into Abby's eyes had reduced him to a stammering idiot. Another minute and he'd have thrown her over his shoulder and dragged her off to the justice of the peace. So much for gradual.

The worst part of all was that the opportunity was wasted. She was back in the city, and if the pictures he'd seen were any indication, she was having the time of her life. How could he ever compete with that?

Having demolished the weed clump, Jarred took the hill in long-legged strides, heading toward the house. The construction crew had completed framing it the day before and the air was filled with the pungent scent of new lumber.

He stared up at the looming skeleton of his dream house and sighed. Without Abby, it would be a nightmare.

His memory burned with the newspaper pictures of Abby and Edward, arm in arm, smiling at one another. Never had he truly considered that she might not one day be his. She was a part of him and they belonged together. Forever.

He sat down hard on the front door frame and buried his face in his hands. "Oh, God, what am I going to do?"

Jarred didn't know how long he stayed that way, but when he finally looked up he felt cleansed and renewed, as he always did after spending time with God. He took a deep breath and released it in a rush.

"Thank You for Your faithfulness, Lord." He pushed himself to his feet and began walking slowly back to his truck. "I hope I don't sound like a complainer," he continued, addressing his statement to the heavens, "when I remind You that I still don't have a clue as to what I'm going to do."

Instantly, Jarred's eyes were drawn to a bright shaft of sunlight that pierced the leafy green canopy of trees overhead and came to rest on the mass of deep green foliage to his right. The bushes seemed to glow from within.

Curious, Jarred walked over to investigate. "Nothing here but blackberries," he said to himself as he stared down into the fruit-laden plants. He swung around and was headed down the hill when suddenly he stopped in mid-stride.

Slowly, his mouth curved into a wide smile.

"Blackberries!"

❧

It was a few minutes after eight when Abigail sat down at her desk and slit open the first envelope in the large stack awaiting her attention and began to read. *Armchair Travel Club Monthly Meeting, Tuesday 7 P.M. City Civic Center. Member physicist Terry O'Conners will share slides from her recent trip to nuclear generators of the world. Promises to be a powerful evening. Refreshments to follow.*

She scooped up the phone at her elbow on the second ring. "Notebook, Bradley."

"Hello, Bradley. Got a minute?"

Abigail's breath caught in her throat at the sound of that velvety smooth voice. "Jarred?"

"Hi, honey," he drawled. "Hope I didn't catch you at a bad time?"

Her heart did a funny little jump and when she tried to speak, her voice came out in a squeak. She cleared her throat and tried again. "No, not at all. I've always got time for a friend. Is there something I can do for you?"

"As a matter of fact, there is. I'm recruiting personnel to harvest my blackberries, and I hoped I could interest you."

"Blackberries?" she asked distractedly, glancing at the calendar on her desk. "Are they ripe already?"

"Yes, ma'am. The bushes are loaded down with them—great big ones this year. The almanac says we're looking at a lot of rain next week, so I wanted to get them picked as soon as possible—say, this weekend."

"This weekend?" She dragged a hand through her hair. "Oh, Jarred, I don't know—"

Jarred's response was immediate. "Look, I understand if you

can't come. I know how busy you are and all. I only mentioned it because I know how much fun we've had picking them in the past. And I'd hate for you to miss out on your mom's cobbler. When I told her I'd be giving you a call she wanted me to be sure and tell you how much they'd love for you to come in."

Abigail's brow arched in amused indignance. "Why do I get the distinct impression that I'm being railroaded?"

"You always were perceptive," Jarred said with a chuckle. "Did it work? Do you think you can make it?"

Abigail leaned back in her chair and closed her eyes. She could hear the smile in Jarred's voice and her imagination was quick to complete the picture with dimples. How could she resist? "Sure, why not?"

&

"I'll tell you why not!" Lurline cried when she heard the news an hour later. "Because Dust Bowl is history. A closed chapter. Not in our plans. It's time to move on. Remember?"

Abigail nodded. She remembered saying each one of those things. And meaning them. "This doesn't change anything, Lurline. It's just a mission of mercy, a harmless little trip to help out an old friend. That's all."

Lurline leaned forward in her chair to thump her long freckled index finger on Abigail's desk. "Harmless mission of mercy, my eye! Jarred's still got dimples, don't he?"

"Well, yes—"

"Then he ain't harmless."

Abigail laughed out loud. "Lurline, you're being silly."

"Maybe so," she replied, her doubtful expression revealing her true opinion, "but it isn't me that's got that weird look back in my eyes." Before Abigail could protest, she added, "I think it's time to regroup."

At the uncharacteristic seriousness of her friend's tone, Abigail pushed back in her chair, folded her arms across her chest, and gave Lurline her full attention.

"First time I met you was a little over a year ago. You wandered into the cafeteria looking like the diagnosis was terminal."

Abigail could almost smile at the memory.

"After you carried your tray to the table in the corner and sat down all by yourself, I came over and asked if you needed a friend."

"Actually," Abigail corrected with a wry grin, "you asked if you could have my pickle."

"Ahem." Lurline fixed her with a mock censorious glare. "Who's telling this story, anyway?"

Abigail stifled a chuckle behind her hand. "Please continue."

"Okay," Lurline said, raising her hands in surrender, "I admit, for the sake of historical accuracy, I asked for the pickle. But it was merely an ice-breaking overture to help put you at ease."

Abigail snorted her disbelief.

"The important thing is, we began to talk. You told me about losing the society page job to someone else and how you were determined you weren't gonna let your rural background be a liability. You said you had a plan. You were going to make something of yourself and nothing was going to get in your way."

"I remember," Abigail said with a wan smile. "I suppose I sounded a bit presumptuous."

"No, not to me." Lurline shook her head, her tight orange curls bobbing furiously. "To my ears, it sounded like a dream come true. You see, what you didn't know was that my life made your life in Dust Bowl look glamorous."

Abigail sat forward in her seat. "Why do you say that? You live here in the city and have a good job."

"My family was too poor to send me to college. I came here to the *Herald* straight from high school because some guidance counselor pulled a few strings."

"Lurline! You never told me—"

Lurline studied her fidgeting hands while she continued. "Talk about your nobodies. I was a poor, uneducated kid from a hick town trapped in dead-end job in Obituaries, that I knew I should be thankful for but wasn't, with the very real prospect of doing the same thing for the next fifty years. It was so depressing. Completely hopeless."

Lurline lifted her clear gaze to Abigail. "Then you came along. You and your big plans for success. And for the first time in my life, I had hope. You said you could make something of yourself and I believed you. For both of us."

"I never knew—"

"Where I come from, folks don't talk about success. They talk about getting by. Surviving. Life is a meaningless treadmill. And until I met you, that's all I had. But you've given me something to believe in. A goal to strive for. A life with meaning and purpose. Success.

"Now here we are a year later, on the precipice of something big. It's really happening just like you said it would. Not necessarily for me," Lurline amended without remorse, "but certainly for you. You've been in the newspaper three times! You're on a first name basis with some highfalutin folks! You're making something of yourself, Abigail, and you can't quit."

Abigail was speechless, humbled right down to the soles of her shoes. She knew Lurline threw herself into "the cause" wholeheartedly, but until now, she didn't know why.

Abigail committed right then and there that she would make something of herself. She would strive just that much harder because Lurline was counting on her. And success would be just that much sweeter.

"I guess the visit won't be a total loss anyway," Lurline added with a shrug.

Something told her she wouldn't want to know, but Abigail asked anyway, "Why do you say that?"

"At least we'll get some answers. I, for one, am dying to find out who will be Jarred's wife."

thirteen

Jarred pushed the brim of his hat back off his forehead with his thumb and swallowed hard. "My wife?" he repeated slowly, as though the term was unfamiliar to him.

"Yes, your wife," Abigail said with the slightest hint of exasperation. "You know, the woman you're building the big house for. The one you're going to marry." *What was* he *looking so uncomfortable about?* Abigail wondered irritably.

Truthfully, she didn't want to bring up the subject of his pending marriage at all; the very thought of it made her heart ache. But she knew Lurline would ask her about it first thing Monday morning and she'd better have the answer.

"Oh, that." Jarred laughed nervously. "I'm glad you asked, Abby." He didn't look very glad as he threaded a finger under his collar. "There's something I've been wanting to tell you."

Abigail raised liquid blue eyes to him and waited. And waited. "Yes?" she prodded.

"I—" he averted his gaze, "I don't want to tell you right now."

It didn't take a genius to figure out that something was wrong. "Jarred, is there a problem?"

He gave a short humorless bark of laughter. "I'll say."

Abigail laid her hand on his arm. "Maybe I can help?"

"Yes." He nodded once before catching himself. "Uh, I mean, no," he amended with a shake of his head. "Look Abigail, the other night when I mentioned I was planning to get married, I spoke prematurely." He shoved his hands in his pockets and studied the ground. "I haven't actually asked her yet—there are some complications."

Abigail's eyes narrowed as she considered her lifelong friend. Jarred was obviously distraught. In all the years she'd known him, she'd never seen him like this before. Jarred was always a rock, a man of supreme confidence. Decisive. Unshakable. So what was going on?

The answer hit her like a ton of bricks. This unknown woman, the one Jarred was going to marry, didn't realize what a treasure she had. Maybe she'd developed cold feet about their relationship and expressed her doubts about their suitability. She had obviously hurt him in some way.

At that moment, something fiercely protective rose up within Abigail. Nobody was allowed to hurt her Jarred. Nobody.

A rush of tenderness swept over her as she studied his strong profile. She raised up on tiptoe to press a quick kiss to his bronzed cheek. "We won't talk about it any more," she promised.

She trotted over to the shady spot where Jarred parked his truck and retrieved the two tin pails from the back. She delivered them into Jarred's hands saying, "Let's pick blackberries."

He remained fixed to the spot. She started running and called over her shoulder, "Race you to the top!"

The surprise challenge seemed to snap Jarred out of his lethargy and he sprinted up the slope behind her. The tall grass and her convulsive laughter impeded her progress and in no time she could hear Jarred's footfalls directly behind her.

They were within fifteen yards of the blackberry patch when he passed her in a burst of speed. After he gained a lead of several feet, he darted into her path and spun around to face her. "The winner!" he cheered, swinging the pails high over his head in a show of victory.

Realization flickered in Jarred's eyes seconds before she plowed into him at top speed, bowling him over and sprawling on top of him in a tangle of arms and legs.

They hit the ground in a whoosh of air and noisy clatter as the tin pails tumbled down the hill.

For a long moment neither spoke. "Jarred?" Abigail whispered finally, hesitant to raise her head from its warm resting place on Jarred's broad chest for fear of what she might find. "Are you okay?"

He didn't answer.

Slowly, fearfully, she looked up, her eyes traveling across his face to assess the damages. It was worse than she had imagined. Jarred's brown eyes were rolled back into his head and his tongue hung limply from the corner of his mouth.

"Jarred?" she gasped. She gripped his broad shoulders and shook him gently. "Jarred, honey?"

Suddenly his eyes rolled forward to meet hers and a wide smile, complete with arresting dimples, covered his face. "Yes?"

Abigail was so relieved, she pounded him on the chest. "You frightened me out of my wits, you, you—"

Jarred easily caught her small pummeling fists in his hand. "I just couldn't resist. I'm sorry."

The humor of the situation struck them simultaneously and they began to laugh. Soon the quiet hillside rocked with their laughter.

"You're sorry?" Abigail hooted between laughs. "I practically killed you and you're apologizing." She turned mirth-filled eyes to Jarred. "I guess that must be the attraction—" Her voice died away as her gaze centered on his. Jarred's hearty laughter broke off suddenly.

From her vantage point, mere inches from his face, she could clearly see the warmth in his dark brown eyes. They seemed to dance with joy and promise. As her gaze traveled over his familiar face, her smile widened. How very precious he was to her.

A sudden, shocking revelation caused her heart to lurch wildly within her chest. She loved him. Abigail swallowed hard. Like a bolt out of the blue, she knew beyond a shadow of a doubt she was in love with Jarred Worth. And there was no denying it— these feelings weren't friendship.

Jarred groaned softly.

At the sound, Abigail snapped back to reality. Her eyes widened with the embarrassing realization she was still sprawled across him.

"Mercy!" she cried. "I must be crushing you!" She wasted no time in scrambling off his large frame and struggling to her feet.

Jarred was on his feet in an instant. "No harm done," he insisted with a dimpled smile as he brushed the grass from his hair.

Her startling new knowledge made her uncomfortable and she refused to meet his eyes. She couldn't be in love with Jarred. She was leaving this part of her life behind. She had the responsibility to make something of herself. "Guess we better get to work," she suggested while resolutely avoiding his gaze. "Time's a wastin'."

☙

Jarred eased back against the wooden slats of the porch swing and sighed with deep contentment. Mrs. Bradley's fried chicken and two helpings of her warm blackberry cobbler went a long way in inducing this kind of euphoria. Of course, Jarred knew it was more.

He knew the sense of rightness he was enjoying at this moment was due largely to having spent the day with Abby. They'd had a wonderful time together—beginning with berry-picking in the cool hours of the morning and ending here on the front porch swing under a starlit sky.

As he stared off into the darkness beyond the porch railing, Jarred's thoughts wandered back to the one mishap in an otherwise perfect day; their collision on Blackberry Hill. What a klutz he'd been. It's a wonder he hadn't killed them both.

A slow smile played at the corners of his mouth. In retrospect, it'd be a lie to say he was sorry for the blunder. After all, the accident afforded him a few moments to hold Abby in his arms.

The memory of their powerful encounter was still fresh on his mind. It was a shame he couldn't harness the energy that coursed through his veins every time he held Abby. Just getting within three feet of her set off enough sparks to light up Tulsa for an entire week.

Even Abby had alluded to an attraction between them. Of course, she was kidding. Jarred frowned slightly. Evidently she didn't share the same incredible sensations he experienced when they were close. Somehow a little word like attraction didn't do justice to the breathlessness he felt when he held her.

At that moment, the subject of his thoughts stepped through the front door with two tall glasses in her hands. "I thought you might like some iced tea," she said as she walked across the porch to join him.

He accepted the frosted glass with a grateful smile. "Thanks, honey."

She settled onto the swing beside him, her shoulder just inches from his. Jarred's long legs moved slightly to propel the swing with gentle motion. They slipped into companionable silence, immersed in the soothing night sounds of chirping crickets and the rhythmic creak of the old wooden swing.

Jarred's arm rested behind Abigail, his finger idly tracing

feather-light patterns on her slender shoulder. A great wave of tenderness washed over him. This was his Abby, the woman he'd been praying for since the day she was born. How right it felt to have her here beside him. He ached to draw her to himself and hold her forever.

Jarred raised his eyes heavenward in silent petition. *How long, Father?* his heart cried out in frustration. *I've prayed faithfully for twenty-two years. How much longer until I see Your answer?*

Abigail seemed blissfully unaware of his turmoil as she released a long sigh. "I haven't had this much fun in a long time, Jarred. Thanks so much for asking me to come."

He toyed with a silken strand of her hair that shone as spun gold in the moonlight. "Have you ever considered coming home, Abby?" It was an effort to keep his tone of voice casual, as though the answer to his question was not of critical importance to him. "I mean, to stay?"

"Sure, I've considered it." She lifted her shoulders in a slight shrug. "But I'm afraid it's out of the question."

Was that regret he heard in her voice? "Why is that?" he asked.

"I'm not going to waste my life. I'm going to make something of myself." She lifted her chin slightly. "I'm going to be a success."

He couldn't resist smiling at her determination. "I don't doubt that for a minute," he assured her. "I just think it would be nice if you did it here at home."

Abigail's heel dug into the floor, abruptly stopping the steady motion of the swing. She turned to him with wide-eyed incredulity. "Make something of myself in Dust Bowl? Ha!"

"Would you mind humoring an old friend and tell me why the concept of becoming a success in Dust Bowl is so funny?"

"Because," she began importantly, then paused to articulate her thoughts, "because success by its very definition is the antithesis of Dust Bowl."

He tilted his brow. "That bad, huh?"

She scowled into his smiling face. "I'm serious, Jarred." Her expression softened slightly as she conceded, "Not that Dust Bowl is a bad place." She seemed to consider him for a moment before dragging her gaze away to study the slatted porch floor. "I truly love it here. I wish—" She cleared her throat. "What I'm trying to say is Dust Bowl is just not the kind of place where you can make something of yourself."

"I had no idea."

She was apparently too wrapped up in her thoughts to hear the amusement in his voice. "Don't be embarrassed, I didn't either. It wasn't until I got to college that I learned the truth."

"What truth is that, honey?"

"The truth that in this world you don't find fulfillment unless you make something of yourself. Something *big*. And nobody achieves anything big in Dust Bowl."

"I guess that all depends on your definition of big."

Abigail rolled her eyes at him. "Big is, well, you know, big is having an important job, high profile if possible. Making a lot of money wouldn't hurt. Big is achieving social prominence and being well-connected with people at the top."

Any humor he found in the conversation died with her last statements. She obviously believed all that garbage. It was his turn to scowl. "Where'd you get a crazy idea like that?"

"Trust me, I didn't go looking for it. It found me. And it isn't so crazy. It was me that was nutty. I was naive enough to believe that my goal of coming back to Dust Bowl and being a wife and mother was real life." She gave a self-deprecating laugh. "I honestly believed raising a family could be challenging and fulfilling."

"And now you don't?"

She shook her head. "No way. I hadn't been to college a full twenty-four hours when I got the facts—double barrel. The dean told me in no uncertain terms that if I wasn't going to be a career woman I was wasting my talents. He explained that if I chose that route for my life, I'd be miserable."

That made Jarred mad. *Where'd this guy get off passing judgment on what Abby did with her life? No wonder she's so confused.* "What kind of—"

Abigail laid a placating hand on his chest. "Now, don't be angry. I admit that at first my feelings were pretty hurt, but actually, the man did me a favor. Imagine how I would have felt blurting out my antiquated ideas in front of my college friends. I would have been the laughingstock of the campus."

"But you don't think everyone feels that way?" Jarred protested.

"I don't think so. I know so."

Abigail raised her hand to silence the argument she could see on his lips. "I don't want you to think it was an isolated event. The kids and faculty at school were only the beginning. It's in the magazines, the television programs—you name it."

"Aw, Abby honey," Jarred cupped her chin with his hand and turned her face to his, "I'm sorry you had to hear all that junk. But you know, just because people are saying something doesn't make it right. Do you know what the Bible says about fulfillment and success? It's the only source of real truth."

She pulled back from his hand and met his eyes evenly. "Jarred, I know the Bible is important to you, and I'm glad for you, but I'm past that part in my life. The Bible is old news. I love God, but I've come to understand that religion is best left out of real life.

"Coming from a small town, we've been insulated from reality, but now, having experienced the real world, I know differently. I'm not going to spend my life as a nothing." She turned her eyes from his. "It's not going to be easy. I've had to make a lot of changes in my life and give up some things I hold dearly. But I will do what I must to find fulfillment and success."

fourteen

Abigail had scarcely switched on her terminal when Lurline bounded up to her cubicle. "Good morning!" she sang out cheerfully as she plopped down in the vacant chair Abigail kept by her desk. "Welcome home, intrepid traveler. When'd you get back?"

"Sunday morning."

"So—did you have a good time?"

"Yeah, I really did. My parents and I played cards till all hours of the night on Friday." She laughed and raised her hands in surrender as if forced into making a confession. "Okay, I admit it was only eleven o'clock when we went to bed, but by Dust Bowl standards that's an all-nighter."

She caught Lurline's grin as she continued, "Saturday we picked four and a half gallons of the biggest, juiciest blackberries you've ever seen, then we went home and baked enough cobbler to feed a small country. By the way, my mom froze one for you. It's in the employee refrigerator."

"I know what I'm having for dinner," Lurline said, smacking her lips in anticipation. She paused for a moment before asking, "How's Dimples?"

"He's fine," Abigail answered noncommittally, working to keep her expression blank. She didn't want her perceptive friend to discover her awful secret. A slight smile tugged at the corner of her mouth. "I can't remember when I've ever laughed so hard." Her gaze returned to Lurline's. "Jarred has a great sense of humor. We always have such a good time together."

Lurline folded her freckled arms across her chest. "And?"

Abigail shrugged. "That's all. We just enjoy being together. Good friends do, you know," she added primly in her own defense.

Lurline studied her face, apparently gauging her sincerity. "You're not thinking of doing anything rash are you?"

Abigail smiled and shook her head. "Not at all. I've got big plans. Remember, I'm a woman with a mission. Success or bust."

Lurline smiled her approval. "Whew! I'm glad to hear it. I was worried about you going home. It's not that I have anything against Dust Bowl, but it seems like after you've been there you come back different." She frowned. "Confused or something." She glanced at her watch. "Say, I've got to get going. My in file is full to overflowing. I guess you could say death is knocking at my door."

Abigail grimaced. "You're so gruesome!"

Lurline gave her best impression of a monster as she slunk away, and Abigail couldn't resist calling out, "See you at lunch, ghoul-friend!"

She could hear Lurline's laughter fading as she disappeared down the corridor. Abigail smiled to herself. She wouldn't forget their mission. She'd make something of herself. She'd find success and fulfillment—for both of them.

She scooped up the stack of mail waiting on her desk. She took a moment to scan each letter before dividing them into piles according to the scheduled date of the activity. It was mindless work which allowed her thoughts to wander.

Lurline didn't need to worry about her being confused any more. No sirree. Everything was crystal clear.

She was head over heels in love with Jarred Worth.

Abigail frowned. She wasn't exactly sure when she slipped over the divide between friendship and love, but she had. She'd inadvertently fallen in love with the one man that could sabotage everything she and Lurline dreamed of.

She couldn't let her feelings get in the way. She'd ignore them, and soon enough they'd fade. At least, she hoped they would.

Lucky for her, Jarred was in love with someone else. She knew it would be difficult to suppress the feelings she had for him, but if he had returned her love, it would be impossible.

The ringing of the phone jarred her attention back to the present. She continued to sift through the letters as she answered, "Bradley, Notebook."

"Abigail? This is Marie, Mr. Robinson's secretary. He asked me to call and set up an appointment with you."

She dropped the pile of mail like a hot potato. "He wants to see me?"

"That's what he said. What's your calendar look like? Any time you could fit him in today or tomorrow?"

Abigail chuckled at the idea that she needed a calendar to keep up with her schedule. "Not much going on down here, Marie," she assured her.

"Are you available at four o'clock?"

"That works for me."

"Great. See you at four."

&

Mr. Robinson rose from his desk when Abigail presented herself at his office door promptly at four. "Welcome, Ms. Bradley. You're right on time. Come in and have a seat, won't you?" he said, motioning toward the chair across the desk from his.

She accepted the seat, remembering the first time she sat there, just a year ago, when she applied for a job with the *Herald*. Mr. Robinson's office struck her now as it did then, rather cramped and sparsely decorated, certainly not what she would expect for the editor of the city's largest paper.

"It's been a long time since we've spoken about your position at the *Herald*, Ms. Bradley. I believe it was the day I hired you, a little over a year ago as I recall."

He peered at her from over the tops of his wire-rimmed glasses. "I've been watching your work in Notebook. And I like what I've seen. The column is straightforward and informative. Top notch reporting to my way of thinking."

Abigail blushed at the unexpected praise.

"That's the reason I wanted to see you today. I've recently been given the go-ahead for a new project and I'd like you to handle it for me."

Abigail forgot all about sophistication. "Me?" she gasped in wide-eyed amazement.

He nodded. "Actually, it's an idea for a new column, something I've been wanting to do for a long time. Public's clamoring for news that isn't blood and guts. You know, they want good news, something folksy. I see it as a logical extension of the Notebook Column."

"I'm sorry, I don't follow. . ."

"It's simple. People submit information to you for publication about public interest events. Why not go one step further and take one such event of your choice each week, subject to management approval of course, and run a story on it? Nothing too elaborate you understand, just a little local interest story."

෪

"Just a little local interest story!" Lurline's whoop of delight split the tomblike silence. She sprang from her desk and threw her arms around Abigail. "Wahoo!" she cried, swinging the two of them in a wide circle. "Wahoo!"

Abigail knew a moment's regret over telling Lurline the news here at the Obituaries desk. Somehow their victory dance looked a bit out of place in an office ordinarily reserved for death.

Lurline, however, felt no such restraint. "This is incredible! I mean it, this is so great!" She swung her friend around again. "You've done it, Abigail! You've got your own byline! Do you know what this means? You're a success!"

fifteen

Abigail rolled over to look at the luminous dial of the clock on the nightstand again. *Five-thirty!* She flopped back against her pillow. Would this miserable night never end?

She had tossed and turned in nervous anticipation of her first interview the entire night. Even now she was half-paralyzed with fear.

She knew there was no point in trying to go back to sleep. Perhaps she should get up and shower and dress for the day. She sat up and swung her feet over the side of her bed. On second thought, if she got dressed this early she'd be hopelessly rumpled for the nine o'clock interview. The downside to a non-synthetic wardrobe was wrinkles. And taking her cues from Suzanne, she was certain wrinkled reporters were not successful reporters.

Her eyes rested on the phone at her bedside. What she needed was someone to talk to. Someone she could tell her worries to. Someone who would listen and make everything all right. Jarred.

Without hesitation she picked up the receiver and dialed his number.

"Hello?"

She smiled at the sleep-gruff sound of his voice. "Jarred? It's me, Abigail. You up?"

"Abby?" The sleepiness in his voice was replaced with concern. "You okay?"

"Yeah." It was true. She felt better just hearing his voice. She lay back against the pillows. "I just wanted to talk."

"What time is it?"

"Five-thirty."

"I gotta tell ya," he confessed with a groggy chuckle, "I don't usually have much to say at five-thirty in the morning, so you start. What's up?"

"I'm doing an interview today. My first. It'll be in the paper on Saturday."

"Hey kid, that's great. I'm proud of you."

He was smiling, she could hear it in his voice. She allowed the pleasure of the sound to wash over her. "I'm really worried though. Everything is riding on the success of this first interview."

"Everything?"

She didn't miss the sarcastic lift of his deep voice. "Well, okay, maybe not everything," she admitted honestly.

She couldn't resist adding, "Just everything that really matters. Like my reputation as a reporter, my status at the paper—" she paused in mid-list. "Let's just say my success in life hinges on the outcome of this morning's interview." Speaking the words brought back the enormity of the task.

"This is the big time, Jarred," she added in a tiny whisper, "and I'm scared."

"Aw, honey, you can do it."

The confidence of his declaration warmed her. "Do you really think so?"

"Know so. You can do anything you put your mind to. Always have. Figure it's that streak of plain mule stubbornness you've got."

She laughed. "Why, Jarred, you always say the nicest things to a girl."

"Just being honest." He yawned. "You'll knock 'em dead, kid. No doubt about it."

"Thanks for talking to me, I feel a hundred times better. Guess I better get going."

"You'll let me know how it goes, won't you?"

"Sure. I'll even send you an autographed copy." She hesitated for a second. "There is one more thing, Jarred."

"Yes?"

"I know what I said about God having no place in the real world, but, I wondered—would you pray for me?"

"Fervently."

"You're the best, Jarred. You really are. I don't know what I'd do without you. Take care. Good-bye."

"Good-bye, honey."

❧

At nine o'clock sharp on the late summer morning, Abigail stepped up to the front door of Mrs. Doris McFarley's home. She paused a moment to inspect her clothing one final time. Perfect. The navy blazer and white pleated skirt looked crisp and professional. Even Suzanne would approve.

Satisfied she was as ready as she'd ever be, she swallowed her nervousness and rapped loudly on the door. From inside the house, she could hear wild barking followed by a sharp voice admonishing, "Pipe down, Itchy. It's the lady from the newspaper."

The door swung open and a hefty woman dressed in her Sunday best stepped into view. "Hello, hello," she greeted in a falsetto voice so sugary it left Abigail wondering if this could possibly be the same person who screeched commands to the dog just seconds before. "You must be the reporter from the *Herald*. I'm Doris McFarley." The small black and white terrier at her side was springing up and down, clearing the floor by six inches in its excitement. "And this is Itchy."

Abigail extended her hand. "Good morning, Mrs. McFarley. I'm Abigail Bradley." The bouncing dog yapped shrilly. "And good morning, Itchy."

"My dear, come inside, won't you. We don't want to waste time out on the porch when we have so much to chat about." Mrs. McFarley moved back into the hall, then stopped. "On the other hand, maybe you should take my picture first," she suggested with a girlish giggle. "I think I photograph best in early morning light."

Abigail was confused. "Picture? Oh, no ma'am. There won't be any pictures with this story."

Gone was the cheery falsetto. "You don't want my picture?"

"It's not that," Abigail was quick to reassure her. "It's just that the editor requested copy only."

"Oh." Mrs. McFarley's animated face sagged with disappointment.

Abigail racked her brain for some sort of concession. "Did I mention the story will be on the front page of the Home and Living section? That's our most desirable placement."

"You don't say." Mrs. McFarley was all smiles once again. "Well, come on in and let's get this interview on the road."

Abigail followed her and Itchy through the modest house to the living room. Her hostess indicated she should sit on the slightly faded sofa.

"I couldn't help but notice all the photographs hanging on the wall as I came in," Abigail said, thinking a little small talk would put Mrs. McFarley at ease. "Are those your children in the pictures?"

Mrs. McFarley nodded enthusiastically. "Three boys and two girls."

"What a large family."

"Yes, it was," Mrs. McFarley agreed, her expression softening at the memory. "And noisy, too. Our house was the one all the neighborhood children gravitated to, so between my five kids and the neighbors, it was a real circus. For a while it seemed that all I did was serve cookies and bandage scraped knees. I guess that must sound just awful to a sophisticated woman like you."

"No ma'am. It sounds wonderful," Abigail admitted wistfully. That had been her dream, devoting her life to raising a big family.

"It was wonderful. There was always something going on; ball games, homework, parties, and school plays." Mrs. McFarley sighed. "I've done a lot of things in my life, but nothing compares to the fun and satisfaction I had raising my family. Do you have any children, Abigail?"

"No." Abigail shook her head. "I'm not married."

"When you are, be sure to have several. Take my word for it, they're a real blessing. It's not an easy job, but I'm certain there isn't another job that's more worthwhile." Mrs. McFarley placed a hand over her heart. "Mercy, I've been rambling, haven't I? Mr. McFarley says that happens when I get excited. I'm so sorry."

"There's no need to apologize. I've enjoyed our conversation," Abigail assured her with a smile. "Maybe now's a good time for me to ask you a few questions, Mrs. McFarley."

"Won't you call me Doodles? All my friends do."

"Yes, thank you—Doodles." Abigail pulled a small notebook from her purse. "As you know, I'm doing a story for the paper on your upcoming family reunion. What I'd like to do is get a few details from you."

"Wonderful. I'm very good with details."

Abigail picked up her pencil. "To begin with, Mrs. McFarley, will you tell me how the idea of having an annual family gathering got started?"

"Doodles."

Abigail looked up from her paper. "I'm sorry?"

Mrs. McFarley looked wounded. "Call me Doodles."

ঌ

Some three hours later, Abigail was seated in front of her terminal, trying to make sense of the four or five pages of notes she'd taken from the interview with Mrs. McFarley—Doodles. Abigail grinned. What an unusual woman. Lucky too. She'd devoted her life to being a wife and mother and didn't seem to suffer from any ill effects.

All in all she thought the interview went really well. Mrs. McFarley was a wellspring of information and more than happy to answer Abigail's questions. It was odd how deferentially she had treated Abigail, as though she were a celebrity. Must be one of the many perks of success.

Abigail circled the salient points in her notes and turned to her keyboard to construct the story that would cinch her success.

McFARLEY CLAN GATHERS FOR ANNUAL FETE

Nearly one hundred McFarleys, representing four generations, will gather this weekend in the City Convention Center for their annual family reunion. Doris "Doodles" McFarley, spokesperson for the clan, says relatives will come from as far away as Texas to attend the gathering.

This year's festivities, which feature games, a talent show, and lots of home cooking will be the twenty-third consecutive reunion for the family.

When asked to pinpoint the single ingredient most responsible for the cohesiveness of these convocations, Mrs. McFarley replied, "The potato salad."

ঌ

"Hi, honey!" Jarred scooped his hat off his head and dumped it along with several rolls of blueprints on top of Abigail's credenza before bending to drop a kiss on her head. "Your article was terrific. First-rate."

"Jarred! I wasn't expecting to see you!" Abigail exclaimed,

clapping a hand over her racing heart. The combination of his sudden appearance and casual kiss left a trail of goose bumps down her arms. She ignored them. "Don't tell me you drove all the way into town just to tell me you liked my story?"

Jarred's mouth pulled into a dimpled grin. "Not exactly. I've got business in town over at the Spa Supply. I thought while I was here I could stop in to see you. Seems I've run into a couple of problems with the house plans, and I'd like your input."

"Problems? Nothing serious I hope?"

"Not at all. It's a matter of built-ins versus windows. Got time to look at it now?"

Thirty minutes later, Jarred rolled up one set of blueprints and tucked it under his arm as he got to his feet. "I've taken up enough of your time this morning. I know you're busy, so I'll get out of your way. He picked up his hat and headed toward the door. "I'm leaving you a set of blueprints to look over when you get a chance. I'll tell the builder to hold off on the windows in the kitchen until I've heard back from you."

He tossed her a warm, dimpled smile. "Thanks for your help, Abby."

"It was my pleasure," she answered a bit breathlessly. "Say, what's at the Spa Supply place, anyway?"

"Paradise." He laughed at her bemused expression. "I was reading about these spas you can have installed in your house. You know, it's a real deep bathtub with all kinds of fancy water jets and stuff. The ad says it's like having an exotic resort in your home. Your own personal paradise. I'm figuring on putting one in the master bathroom."

Abigail unrolled her set of blueprints and located the master bath with her fingertip. "Jarred?"

He cocked a brow in question.

"I'm looking at the dimensions of this bathtub you're talking about." She furrowed her brow as she studied the blue lines. "There must be some mistake here. It says forty-eight by sixty inches. That's enormous." She lifted her gaze to his. "Do you realize that's big enough for two people?"

He dropped his hat on his head. "Yes ma'am, I do."

sixteen

"Did you miss me?"

Abigail drew a blank. "Miss you?"

Edward looked wounded. "In case you hadn't noticed, it's September fifteenth. I've been out on the West Coast for the past four days."

"Of course I noticed," she answered with an easy smile. "It's just that you're normally out of town a couple of days each week, so I'm used to it."

He reached over to take her hand. "Do you mind?"

"Not at all." She met his gaze squarely. "We both know success doesn't come without a price."

Edward considered her for a long moment. "You're an unusual woman, Abigail. You have the most uncanny ability to cut to the heart of a matter. There are precious few people who have such a clear understanding of the important things in life."

She lowered her eyes at the praise. "Thank you."

"I've always said the essence of life is composed of our accomplishments and our possessions, but it's rare to find someone who shares the same vision." He contemplated the glass in his hand for a moment before adding, "The true measure of a man or woman is ultimately what he or she has achieved." He drank deeply of the amber liquid. "Success is everything."

Abigail winced inwardly. For a split second, she felt uneasy about the words he spoke. True, they were the very thoughts she'd been espousing for months. But, somehow, hearing them articulated by Edward in his very elegant, slightly nasal voice didn't make them sound quite so appealing.

She brushed aside the notion as another silly doubt, obviously a product of her small town upbringing. After all, every magazine, newspaper, and television show wouldn't proclaim the message that success was measured in tangibles if it weren't true.

She had only to look around to get her answer. What kind of people were admired and emulated in the world? Was it the devoted mother, the poor but honest laborer, or the pious Christian? No indeed. It was the rich and powerful.

A waiter appeared at their tableside with a platter heaped with long spindly crab legs. A second waiter followed in his wake with bowls of drawn butter and the hardware required to retrieve the crabmeat.

"You are going to love these," Edward promised. "Antoine's has the freshest seafood in the city. Anytime they offer crab legs on the menu, I jump at the chance to get them."

As the staff busied themselves with the preparations which included tying a plastic bib around Abigail's neck, she glanced around the restaurant. For the first time that evening, she actually took notice of her surroundings.

Flickering candlelight, soft music, gleaming silver, and crisp white linen. Funny, the things that used to impress her had now become commonplace. Over the months she'd been seeing Edward, and been exposed to such opulence, it had become second nature to her.

A self-satisfied smile curved her mouth. She'd done it. Her efforts to cultivate a demeanor of worldly sophistication finally paid off. She had arrived.

"Are you ready for the epicurean experience of a lifetime?" With her nod Edward proceeded to instruct her in the proper way to eat crab legs. "Hold the leg in your left hand, like this. Break it here at the joint with the pliers," he clamped the shiny stainless steel tool around the leg and squeezed, "and pull the meat out with your fork. Dip it in the butter and eat."

Abigail followed his instructions to the letter. In no time at all, the leg lay splintered on her plate and a tiny morsel of crabmeat dangled from the tine of her fork.

"Go ahead," Edward prompted. "Dip it in the butter."

Again, she did as she was told, dredging the minuscule clump of meat in the bowl of butter and popping it into her mouth.

"Well?" He watched as she chewed. "How is it?"

Her honest appraisal would be that it was an awful lot of work for nothing, but she replied graciously, "Delicious."

Forty-five minutes later, the plate in front of her was stacked high with leg fragments, and her appetite as yet unappeased.

Edward pushed his plate away with a sigh of satisfaction. "So what did you think of them?"

Abigail picked up a disembodied leg and wagged it in his direction. "I've come up with a theory about these crab legs. I bet some fella was sitting around one day trying to figure out a way to stretch his profit from crabs. Folks are always clamoring for the claws where the meat is and throwing the rest away."

She set the leg back on the plate. "This guy figures that if he tells people the legs are a delicacy, and charges them exorbitant prices to prove it, he'd make a little money on the throw-aways."

It was always a bit unnerving to have Edward's full attention, as she did now. He had a way of looking at her, an unblinking stare, that made Abigail a bit uncomfortable. Had she said something wrong?

Suddenly, Edward began to chuckle. "I don't know where you come up with these things, Abigail." He laughed as he shook his head. "Your sense of humor is priceless!"

There it was again. Her sense of humor. A day didn't go by that somebody didn't comment on how funny she was.

She didn't correct Edward. Better he think her witty than know for a fact she was a backward yokel from Dust Bowl. She needed to learn to check those annoying impulses to speak her mind.

Abigail smoothed the linen napkin in her lap. *Other than an occasional inappropriate outburst,* she reassured her slightly damaged pride, *I've mastered the whole sophistication thing quite neatly.*

The waiter removed the plate of crab carnage from Abigail's place and left a bowl of steaming clear liquid in its stead. She smiled her thanks at his thoughtfulness. He must have suspected the platter of crab claws wouldn't fill her up and brought her a supplemental bowl of broth.

She picked up her spoon and began to eat. Rather tasteless, she thought, taking another spoonful. The lemon slice floating in the bowl gave no clue as to the flavor.

Edward was laughing again. "You are such a clown."

It was then she noticed him whishing his fingers around in the similar bowl of liquid at his place. She dropped her spoon with a self-conscious laugh and followed his example.

His eyes sparkled with laughter. "Drinking out of the finger bowl! Where do you come up with these things?"

❧

Abigail dug her fork into the rich, three-layer fudge cake. She took advantage of the brief lull in interruptions to taste the delicious confection. She sighed with pleasure.

"That good?" Edward asked.

"Heavenly."

"For a while there I didn't think you'd get a chance to eat it."

Abigail smiled. "We have had an awful lot of company this evening. Maybe we should've stayed at the restaurant for dessert instead of coming to the club."

"Nonsense, dessert at the club has become a tradition with us."

Even as they spoke, a woman in her late twenties approached their table. "Oh, Abigail, I'm so glad you're here." She seemed to notice Edward as an afterthought. "Hello, Edward. Good to see you."

"Hi, Denise." Abigail smiled warmly. "Won't you sit down and join us for some dessert?"

"I'd love to but I can't stay. I just wanted to tell you I took your advice and skipped the belt." She pointed to her waist. "You were so right. The outfit makes so much more of a statement without it." Denise turned to Edward. "Abigail has such a knack with this sort of thing."

Denise bent to press her cheek to Abigail's in what Abigail laughingly described to Lurline as the "Country Club Clinch."

"Gotta run. Let's do lunch sometime." She waved to Edward and disappeared through the door.

Edward was obviously impressed. "I had no idea yours was the last word in fashion."

"Funny, isn't it?" Abigail said with a shrug. "My association with you over the past few months has done wonders for my credibility. Suddenly I find myself sought out for my fashion advice from people who would never have noticed me except for the fact that I'm with you."

"That may be true," Edward conceded, "but I think Denise is correct. You do have a knack."

Abigail laughed, brushing off his compliment. "So I've heard. For making something from nothing."

Abigail rolled over and squinted at the alarm clock by her bed. *Three-oh-six.* She flopped onto her back with a sigh. She'd been lying there a full two hours courting sleep to no avail.

Her thoughts whirled with images of the evening. Edward's elegantly handsome face glowing with warm approval over her concept of success, spidery white crab legs stacked high on fine china platters, and society's darlings stopping by her table to ask her fashion advice. What a night. She'd sure come a long way from her Dust Bowl roots.

She wondered absently as she stared at the darkened ceiling how her accomplishments stacked up against the list she and Lurline compiled months ago when they first began their quest for success.

Her new job certainly fit the bill for success. She was a full-fledged reporter now with a public to interview and deadlines to meet. Her last paycheck reflected a significant raise and she'd received two fan letters!

Her possessions were shaping up nicely. Sure, her car wasn't an expensive import, but her wardrobe was the envy of all her peers. The girls at the *Herald* positively swooned over the impressive designer labels she was wearing and Oklahoma's jet set waited with bated breath to catch a glimpse of her latest interpretation of simple elegance.

Then there was her social status. No complaints there. In fact, her social calendar was the stuff dreams were made of. Galas, theater, the most chic entertainment—all under the escort of the city's most eligible bachelor and documented by her almost weekly appearances in the society pages.

Not bad. Not bad at all. She closed her eyes and pulled the covers up more tightly under her chin. Suddenly, her eyes flew open and she bolted upright in bed. *Not bad?* What an understatement! It was incredible. She'd done it! In a few short months, she'd transformed herself from a nobody to a real somebody. *I'm a success!*

The clock read four-thirteen. Exhaustion was finally claiming Abigail and her last thought before dropping off to sleep was a troubling one. *If this is what I've been searching for—why doesn't it feel like enough?*

seventeen

Lurline pressed carefully into the crowd of people milling around Abigail's desk, balancing a cup of steaming coffee in each hand. It was no use. She couldn't get through. Even though her friend's new cubicle was larger than the one she'd occupied down in the "catacombs," it wasn't large enough to accommodate this many visitors.

"Make way! Coming through!" No response. "Haven't you people got anything better to do?" Lurline muttered under her breath. Sudden inspiration put a mischievous smile on her face as she pronounced, "Say, isn't that the supervisor I see coming this way?"

The party dispersed in a heartbeat. Lurline waited until the last body disappeared down the corridor before she commandeered the chair beside Abigail. "Howdy stranger. Got time to have a cup of coffee with your pal?"

Abigail grinned. "Sounds great." She accepted the cup from Lurline. "You've got a real gift for crowd control."

"Thanks."

Abigail sipped the steamy brew. "How's things downstairs in Obituaries?"

"Business is booming. But you won't hear me bragging about it."

Abigail was suspicious. "And why is that?"

"We both know death be not proud."

Abigail groaned. "Where do you come up with that stuff?"

"Just another of my gifts." Lurline took a long draught from her cup. "But hey, that's enough about me. How's your life? Not that I can't guess. After all, I saw that fabulous picture of you and Edward at the gala in Sunday's paper." Lurline whistled. "Talk about a picture being worth a thousand words."

Abigail was perplexed. "I'm sorry? Maybe it's because I haven't had my caffeine yet, but I don't know what you're talking about."

"No need to be coy. I'm referring to the steamy picture that the whole world saw of the perfect society couple sharing an inti-mate moment." At the look on Abigail's face she continued,

"Don't try to deny it. It was all there in black and white. Your heads together, Edward whispering something in your ear." Lurline wiggled her eyebrows. "I've been dying to know what he was saying."

"Oh *that* intimate moment!" Abigail exclaimed with new understanding. She scooted her chair closer to Lurline's and lowered her voice to a sultry whisper. "He said, 'Turn your head slightly to the right. You'll get a better picture if you don't look directly into the flash.'" She leaned back to add wryly, "Intimate and practical."

"You're kidding, right?"

Abigail slowly shook her head.

Lurline was genuinely crestfallen. "You're not kidding?" She held her disappointed silence for a moment. "Well, okay, so it wasn't an intimate moment, but don't try to tell me that the gala wasn't the most fun you've ever had. This is the culmination of your climb to success, mingling with society giants. It must have been the highlight of your life."

"I thought it would be," Abigail admitted with an embarrassed shrug. "And it was okay—"

"Okay? Just okay? Attending the social event of the year with the bachelor of the year was just okay?"

Abigail accepted Lurline's screeched protest as her due. "I don't know what's wrong with me. The gala was the kind of party a girl dreams of all her life. I bought a terrific new dress, had my hair professionally styled—I even got these acrylic nails put on!" She extended her hands to Lurline for inspection.

Lurline studied the enameled nails with awe. "Cool."

"But, in spite of my hopes, it just wasn't great."

"Define 'wasn't great.' "

Abigail tried to put into words the feelings of emptiness and futility she'd been struggling with over the last few weeks. "I don't know. Maybe I'm crazy. I mean, it was all very elegant. The club was decorated with a zillion candles and fresh flowers—it looked like something out of a fairy tale."

"Wow."

"And Edward did introduce me to all of his friends, which was nice. Did you know he's personal friends with the governor?"

"That is so cool."

Abigail concentrated on the positive. "The dressing up was fun, and Edward was nice. I met an awful lot of very influential people, but truthfully, I was glad when it was over."

Lurline threw up her hands. "You're right. You're crazy!"

"I must be, because it looked to me like everyone else there felt the same way I did. Sure they were going through the motions and polite chitchat, but they all looked...I don't know...bored."

"Bored? Don't be ridiculous. Have you ever read a single society column that referred to bored guests?"

"Well—"

"Of course not! It doesn't happen!"

"Maybe you're right. I did notice Deidre Harrington seemed to be having a great time. Suzanne says she's always the life of the party."

"See there!" Lurline pounced on her statement. "You just need to find out her secret."

Abigail considered the idea. "I guess I could ask Suzanne. I'm having lunch with her today."

"Perfect! If anybody knows how to thrive in society it's Miss High-and-mighty."

æ

Suzanne tapped the crystal of her diamond encrusted watch impatiently. "You're late."

"I know." Abigail slid into the empty chair at the table that was conspicuously located in the center of the large dining room. "I'm truly sorry. I've been circling the parking lot for fifteen minutes looking for a parking space."

"Abigail, Abigail." Suzanne clucked her tongue. "You can take the girl out of Dust Bowl, but you can't take the Dust Bowl out of the girl," she said with a rueful shake of her head. "That's why we have valets, dear."

In spite of Suzanne's convictions to the contrary, Abigail knew all about valets. They were a wonderful uniformed convenience that worked for tips. Tips. That was the problem. With all the expenses she'd incurred in preparation for the gala, she had precious little money left to hold her over until payday. She certainly could not afford to fritter any away on luxuries. Not that she'd ever admit it to Suzanne.

Time for a diversion. Abigail scooped the menu off the table and scanned the contents. "So, what are you going to order?"

The tactic worked. "I hear the mushroom quiche is divine."

❧

"This is good," Abigail remarked enthusiastically around her first bite of quiche. "Really delicious." She'd ordered the mushroom quiche to placate Suzanne. Personally, she wasn't sure why people made such a big deal about eating anything that looked like toadstools. Folks back in Dust Bowl wouldn't give two hoots for a whole bush of the nasty things. But here in the city people craved them. Must be something like the crab leg thing.

"So, what did you think of our little gala Saturday night?"

Caught off guard, Abigail racked her brain for an honest, yet positive reply. "It was—nice." Her attention was focused on her fingertips tracing the edge of her iced tea glass. "Elegant, well-decorated—"

"In other words, a dead bore."

Abigail's head snapped up. "I'm sorry?"

"You heard me, I said it was a dead bore. It's a well-known fact, the gala is deadly dull." Suzanne studied her nails before looking up at Abigail, "Although I must admit, I'm terribly surprised someone like you would notice. Sometimes I think there's hope for you yet."

The backhanded compliment rolled off her back. "I must be missing something. You're saying everyone knows the gala is a bore?"

"Certainly. We dread it for an entire year."

"If everyone dreads it, then why do they bother to have one again the next year?"

"You say the funniest things." Suzanne chuckled dryly. "We hold the gala year after year because it's the thing to do. You know, a see and be seen sort of event."

"Well, sure I knew that," Abigail bluffed. "However," she added in an attempt to look knowledgeable, "I'm not so sure everyone dreads it. It looked like Deidre Harrington was enjoying herself."

"She was, wasn't she?" Suzanne shrugged disinterestedly.

"But then, she always does."

Abigail leaned forward in her chair to pose her next question. The answer was critical. The secret to Deidre's happiness might well be the final step Abigail needed to take to derive fulfillment from her newfound success. "Why do you suppose that is? Why does Deidre always have a good time?"

"She's drunk."

Abigail fell back against her seat. "Drunk?" she repeated in a stunned whisper.

Suzanne nodded her affirmation.

"I had no idea."

"Well, then, you're the only one. Fact is, I haven't seen Deidre Harrington sober in years."

"I don't understand," Abigail said, shaking her head. "Why would someone like Deidre drink?"

"That's easy. She's miserable."

"She can't be!" Abigail blurted out, in spite of her determination to be cool and sophisticated. "She has everything!"

Suzanne quirked a heavily penciled brow. "So?"

"So—she's a success."

"You're absolutely correct," Suzanne replied. "Deidre Harrington is every inch a success. But that has nothing to do with happiness or fulfillment."

Suzanne's casual statement sent Abigail's mind reeling. What did she mean that success didn't have anything to do with happiness? A horrible thought resurfaced in her mind. *What if she's right? What if success isn't enough?*

Frantic to silence the doubt once and for all, Abigail glanced around the bustling restaurant. Her glance came to rest on the perfect example of satisfied success. "There's Mary Alice Munson over there with her decorator. Now there's a woman who has it all."

"She seems to think so right now," Suzanne agreed. "But, of course, she always feels that way when she's taken a new paramour."

Abigail paled visibly.

"You didn't know?" Suzanne laughed. "Now don't tell me you actually believed that Vancinti was with her night and day just to rearrange her furniture?"

"Well, yes."

Suzanne was obviously enjoying Abigail's discomfort. "You country girls are so naive."

"But her husband—"

Suzanne cut her off. "Her husband has had a whole string of liaisons, so you needn't be outraged." She shrugged. "It's just the way of things."

The situation was going from bad to worse. Instead of quieting her fears with reassurance that those with success were happy and fulfilled, Suzanne's statements were adding new horrors to her previous doubts.

Abigail took Suzanne's hand, ignoring the startled look on the other woman's face. "But you, Suzanne," her voice was almost pleading, "you're happy, aren't you?"

"Happy?" Suzanne considered the question for a moment. "Yes, I believe I am."

Abigail released her hand and sighed in relief.

"After fifteen years of therapy, I feel like I can finally say, I'm happy. At least some of the time." Suzanne paused to qualify herself. "I mean, Dr. Whatley says I'm happy, and he should know. He's a genius."

"Dr. Whatley?" Abigail asked weakly.

"My psychiatrist. You know, my shrink." She glared at Abigail. "You needn't look so surprised. Everyone sees one." She paused to study Abigail. "Come to think of it, you should see Dr. Whatley."

Abigail shook her head vehemently. "I don't think so—"

"Nonsense," Suzanne said with an easy wave of her hand. "It's a great idea. I don't know why I didn't think of it sooner." She considered Abigail. "Just look at you. I don't think I've ever noticed it before, but you're a bundle of nerves. Trust me, a little delving into your psyche and Dr. Whatley will have you fixed up in no time."

eighteen

"Any place a hungry traveler could get some lunch around here?"

"Abby!" Jarred sprang to his feet. "I didn't know you were coming home this weekend."

She ran a hand through her hair. "I didn't either." She smiled vaguely. "It was just one of those last minute ideas."

Her mother swept her into her arms. "We're not so foolish as to question a blessing. We're just tickled pink you could make it." She bustled Abigail into the kitchen. "Come sit down, won't you. Samuel, you and Jarred need to put away your papers until after lunch."

Intrigued, Abigail watched as her father and Jarred cleared away their things.

"Your daddy and Jarred are planning to build me a new greenhouse," she explained proudly.

Abigail helped her mother make sandwiches and stew, and relaxed as the four of them settled at the table.

After the blessing Samuel took a large helping of stew and passed the bowl to Abigail. "So darlin', how's every little thing in the big city?"

"Great," she said without meeting his eyes, passing the bowl on to Jarred. "Work is keeping me busy. Mr. Robinson seems very pleased with my column. We've gotten enough positive feedback that management has upgraded us from trial to permanent status."

"Oh, Abby, that's just wonderful. Not that I'm the least bit surprised. Why just the other day Maudine Wilson called to tell me that your article on fly fishing brought tears to her eyes. 'Course, I know she tends to get a bit emotional, but the point is that you're touching people's hearts with your column."

"That's the truth," her father added. "Folks were just plain tired of reading nothing but bad news."

The conversation flowed easily. Her parents and Jarred positively bubbled with enthusiasm about her work at the paper. If anyone noticed that Abigail was unusually quiet, they didn't say so. A smile or nod from her at the appropriate times seemed to satisfy them.

She wasn't certain it had been a good decision to come home. Lurline wouldn't think so. But after yesterday's lunch with Suzanne, Abigail needed some time away. Some time to think.

Warm sunlight streamed through spotless windows into the cheery yellow kitchen. How many times had she looked at this room over the last two years and groaned inwardly at how hopelessly outdated it was. The chrome and Formica table they were gathered around was so old it was on the verge of making a comeback as an antique. The goldenrod priscilla curtains in the windows screamed seventies.

Suddenly she was thankful she hadn't pressed her mother to change it. It felt good to sit back and soak up the comforting atmosphere of home. She sighed.

The conversation stopped. "Abby? You all right?"

"Me?" Her eyes widened with the realization that she'd sighed aloud. "Sure," she replied, nodding with undue force. "Fine. Really."

She was relieved when they paused only briefly before picking up where they left off. Another lie. She wasn't all right. She was all wrong. For the second time in her life, her foundation was crumbling beneath her.

The first time, in college when her lifelong beliefs were challenged, was difficult. But, at least, the professors replaced what they took. Their real-world perspective of success fit nicely where her antiquated notions of God and family once stood.

This time, her rock solid conviction that social and financial success was the source of happiness and fulfillment was being shaken out from under her and there wasn't a net.

If success was a lie, God outdated, and home and family a trap—what was left?

She glanced at the people around the table and smiled. In a world of change and upheaval, these beloved people remained constant. Her gaze slipped to Jarred. Strong, solid Jarred. A rock in turbulent waters. On second thought, she was awfully glad she'd come home.

❧

Abigail rinsed the last of the dishes and handed it to Jarred to dry.

"Hey kid," he said, as he swiped the towel over the plate and stacked it in the cabinet with the others, "Whaddya say we head up to Blackberry Hill? You won't believe how great the place is coming along."

❧

Jarred pulled his truck to a stop and switched off the ignition. Abigail's troubles were momentarily forgotten as she stared up at the impressive two-story structure perched on the hilltop. "My heavens, Jarred! It's a house!"

Jarred chuckled. "Hadn't I told you that's what I was planning to build all along?" He rubbed his jaw as if truly puzzled.

She dismissed his teasing with an impatient wave of her hand. "Very funny. I knew what you were building. It's just that I didn't expect it to look like a house—not yet anyway. I mean it's got a roof already, and glass in the windows and—"

"Whoa there, don't get too excited. We're still a ways off." He swung out of the truck and called to her, "Let's go in and I'll show you around."

They trooped across the grass and climbed the brick stairs. Jarred pushed open the unpainted door and stepped aside for Abigail to enter.

Abigail's gaze swept the entry hall from floor to ceiling. "Wow!" Jarred was correct. There was still much to do inside. The walls were sheets of unadorned drywall and the concrete floors were littered with sawdust and nails. Yet, even in its present state, Abigail could appreciate the soaring ceilings and graceful proportions they'd created from sketches on paper.

She followed him into the dining room. "Oh, Jarred!" Abigail clasped her hands together. "Look at all the light!" Sunlight streamed through the enormous arched windows and flooded the room with its brilliance. "It's wonderful!"

Jarred grinned with obvious pride. "Somehow I knew you'd be an appreciative audience."

And she was. The reality of the house, seeing the actual building, far surpassed her fondest dreams. She wandered excitedly from room to room, exclaiming over the beauty of some feature, proclaiming another to be a stroke of pure genius. Her heart swelled with pride. With the time and planning she'd invested in the house, it felt very much like her own.

"Now we come to the master bedroom," Jarred said. "You're gonna love this."

Abigail stepped back suddenly. "It's very nice, I'm sure." She spared it a quick glance before turning and hurrying down the hall. "Say, have they finished the fireplace in the living room yet?" she called over her shoulder.

Jarred trotted up behind her and grabbed her shoulders. "Wait a minute, Abby. You're getting ahead of the tour." He turned her around and directed her back toward the master bedroom. "I want to show you some changes I made in the closets."

He half-dragged her across the room into the enormous bathroom. Two cavernous closets flanked the space where the paradise tub would later be installed. He ducked into the one on the right. "Look." He pointed toward a chest of drawers that was built into the wall. "It's cedar, for storing sweaters and wool stuff."

Abigail tried to match his enthusiasm with a smile of her own. "Terrific."

Jarred had moved out of the closet and was explaining something about the glass-block shower, but Abigail didn't wait to comment. Instead, she practically ran out of the bedroom and down the hall, not stopping until she came to the front door. She dropped down to sit in the open doorway, pulling her knees close to her chest.

"Hey, kid?" She could hear Jarred's boots crunching on the cluttered floor as he came toward her. He nudged her aside to make room to sit on her left. He lifted her chin in his hand and studied her face for a moment. "Something wrong, Abby?"

"Nothing." She shook her head. "Why do you ask?"

"One minute you're praising every board and nail in the place and the next minute you're racing out like the place is on fire."

She shrugged. "You've seen one closet, you've seen them all."

Jarred didn't reply and the two lapsed into silence. Abigail's eyes were trained on some distant spot, but her thoughts tossed about in every direction.

What was wrong with her? Why had the tour suddenly soured for her? One minute she was strolling through the rooms expounding on the many wondrous features and mentally arranging furniture, and the next minute she felt like a trespasser frantically trying to escape. It didn't make sense.

She loved the house. Walking through the sunlit spaces she could easily imagine the loving, boisterous family that would grow up within its walls. It made her smile to think of the rooms echoing with love and laughter.

Then they got to the master bedroom and a sudden chill swept over her. This house was not hers. She had no part in the love and laughter. Jarred built the house for his wife. The woman he loved. *I don't belong here.*

It hurt to think about it. It was easy to say she'd be satisfied to ignore her true feelings for him and to have him as a friend, but much harder to put into practice. Jarred was so easy to love.

But it could never be. Even if Jarred loved her, she would not return his love. She had chosen to leave this all behind in favor of life in the city and she couldn't turn back now. She had to find success and fulfillment. Everything depended on that.

"So, are you going to tell me about it?"

Abigail blinked back the hot moisture from her eyes. "About what?"

"Whatever it is that's bothering you." Jarred's gaze pierced hers. "I've known you too long to fall for that innocent act. You and I both know you don't come hightailing it back to Dust Bowl just to eat lunch with the natives. And I s'pect that big city society page is going to be blank if you aren't there doing something to write about."

She shot him a startled look. "You read the society pages?"

He shrugged his broad shoulders negligently. "Only if I don't have anything better to do." He scowled. "And don't try to change the subject. I want to know what's bothering you. You gonna 'fess up willingly or do I have to tickle it out of you?"

The familiar threat brought a smile to her face. "It's nothing. Really."

Jarred cocked a brow. "Somebody bothering you? Do I need to come straighten things out?"

She laughed in spite of herself. "Like you straightened out Berle Beaudecker?"

"Aw, Abby, that was a long time ago. Don't you forget anything?" He rolled his eyes at her. "Never mind grinning at me like that. You know he needed it. Don't know what got into Berle to make him talk like that in front of you. I was just refreshing his manners."

"And rearranging his face."

"If you will recall, Miss Memory, he thanked me later. Said I knocked some sense into him."

"I've always thought the hump on his nose gave him character."

"I've never heard his wife complain."

At the mention of the word wife, Abigail sobered. "You don't need to worry. Nobody's bothering me. I'm just a little—unsettled, that's all. I came home to do some thinking. You know, regain my perspective."

Jarred smiled broadly before wrapping a big arm around her shoulders and pulling her close. "Home's a mighty fine place for finding perspective."

Abigail allowed herself the luxury of enjoying his friendly gesture and rested her head against his shoulder. The Oklahoma sun shone warm on her face and the morning breeze stirred her hair.

Sitting there on the hilltop, high above the noise and bustle of humanity below, and securely nestled in Jarred's strong arms, she felt strangely powerful. Invincible. She was confident she could solve all the world's problems. She supposed, reluctantly, that she should start with her own.

Her immediate problem was one of concentration. She had Jarred to thank for that. His nearness was having a particularly distracting effect on her mind this morning.

For one thing, he smelled so nice—that soapy clean, Jarred-y smell that was his alone—that she didn't want to think at all. She was quite content to sit and sniff.

And with her head resting against his strong chest, his crisp shirt rubbing her cheek, she found herself satisfied to fill her thoughts with nothing more than the lovely, steady thudding of his heart.

Unfortunately, enjoying Jarred's nearness was getting her nowhere. Tomorrow she was heading back for the city and she needed answers. Now.

Actually, her problem was not a complex one. Very simply, she was looking for the truth.

She had achieved all the things the world said made her a success. Certainly there were many others who had achieved more, but there was no denying her own success. Yet the promised satisfaction and fulfillment did not come. Her deep need for purpose in life was not met. While all her accomplishments were very nice, she was empty.

And she was not alone. Suzanne, Mary Alice Munson, and Deidre Harrington were all women who met and surpassed the prescribed requirements for success, yet they, too, were empty. It didn't take a genius to figure out that drinking, adulterous relationships, and years of therapy were devices these women employed to fill their voids. The same void that yawned within Abigail.

She wondered how many others were like them. People who looked successful and satisfied on the outside, but inside their lives were in shambles.

"You got time to stay for church tomorrow?" Jarred's deep voice penetrated her musings. "I know for myself that a dose of praise and worship helps me get things into perspective."

*

Jarred was right. His advice to attend church was just the tonic she needed. She sat on the pew between her mother and father and reveled in the peace and tranquility she always found in the house of God. Her spirits soared. This time she had the full formula for success. All she had to do was find the right church in the city.

nineteen

"You're looking awfully cheerful for a Monday morning," Lurline accused as she placed a cup of coffee on Abigail's desk and sank into the empty chair beside her. "Care to share your secret?"

Abigail smiled. "No secret. You're looking at a woman who's been refreshed by a weekend of R and R at home."

"Home?" Lurline screeched. "You went to Dust Bowl?"

Abigail raised her palms to quiet her friend. "I was afraid you'd react this way. Calm down, won't you? It was no big deal. I just wanted to get away."

"I'll be the judge of whether it was a big deal or not." Lurline fixed her with a withering stare. "Was Jarred there?"

Abigail shrugged. "Yeah."

"Then it was a big deal."

"Not at all. I didn't go to see him. I merely went home to do a little thinking. Like I said, no big deal."

Lurline was obviously not convinced. "So what was the outcome?"

"The outcome is that I am zeroing in on the secret of total success. The sense of completion, of true fulfillment is within my grasp." Abigail took a sip of the steaming coffee. "Have I mentioned to you how wise Jarred is?"

Lurline rolled her eyes. "Honestly, Abigail, don't you ever get tired of talking about that guy?"

"Don't be silly. I rarely bring up his name. I only mention him now because after this weekend I have a new appreciation of the depth of his wisdom." She paused to taste her coffee again. "You know, Lurline, Jarred's a very perceptive man, the kind of person that is gifted with a true understanding of human nature."

"Abigail, you're making me sick."

Abigail ignored the caustic remark. "He was the one that tipped me off to the missing element in our success formula."

"Oh he did? And exactly what is the missing element?"

"Church attendance."

"I'm sorry?"

"You heard me, I said church attendance. Don't look so

124

shocked. It makes perfect sense. I've been wondering why after accomplishing all the things needed to become happy and successful, that I'm not. Happy, that is. Jarred reminded me that going to church gives balance to one's life."

"I never thought of it that way before."

"Me either. Funny that we'd miss something so obvious." She lifted her shoulders. "No harm done. We're on the right track now. Going to church is the right thing to do."

❊

"I don't believe I've ever seen a church quite this big before," Abigail whispered while doing her best not to gawk openly at the palatial structure. It appeared the church foyer alone could hold several hundred people.

Edward gave a regal nod. "Quite impressive, isn't it? It's the largest in the city. I believe it was built some twenty years ago after First Church downtown split."

"The church split?"

"Not literally, of course. Some sort of nasty congregational dispute from what I hear. It seems there was a trouble-making faction within the church. You know—the ultra religious type. They were trying to force the leadership to abandon their social messages and adopt a policy of strict adherence to Scripture."

Abigail nodded.

"Luckily, the leadership realized their responsibility to the community and opted to retain their socially responsible emphasis."

"What happened to the troublemakers?"

Edward shrugged disinterestedly. "They kept the old building, the one over on the corner of Madison and Sixteenth. As far as I know, they're still preaching outdated ideas to their little flock of fanatics."

"It's a small church, then?"

"No doubt." Edward was clearly bored discussing the infidels. "The majority of the church sided with the leadership. It's to their credit that they had the foresight to build this new facility on prime real estate. It's a far better reflection of the clientele they serve."

By this time, Abigail and Edward had inched their way along with the crowd to the back of the sanctuary. She looped her arm through Edward's and followed the usher over carpet so impossibly thick she worried she might lose a shoe in it. As she high-stepped down the aisle, she was struck by the tomblike silence in the sanctuary. It was especially eerie considering the number of people sitting in the pews. There was no cheerful banter or even whispering among the congregation. It seemed to Abigail that all eyes were on them, watching their slow progress down the aisle.

Finally, the usher stopped when they'd reached the third row from the front. He extended his arm, indicating they were to sit. Abigail smiled gratefully before slipping into the row and sinking down onto the luxuriously upholstered pew. She sat back and folded her hands in her lap, fearing any undue movement might attract more attention to them. Moving only her eyes, she surveyed the sanctuary.

Unlike her little church in Dust Bowl that was a cheery jumble of color and pattern, everything in First Church was perfectly coordinated in white, powder blue, or gold. Heavy on the white.

The towering walls, lofty arched ceilings, and rows of pews were swathed in a blanket of pristine white. The floors and pew seats were covered in an elegant shade of powder blue, and any extras, the altar, light fixtures, and incidentals, were done in opulent gold.

Whewee! I wonder who God uses as a decorator?

Abigail's eyes flew open in horror. She did it again! Why was it that every time she opened her mouth she put her foot in it? A quick glance toward Edward reassured her that her foolish comment had not been spoken aloud. She smiled to herself. Her self-control was coming along nicely. *Who says you can't take the Dust Bowl out of the girl?*

Promptly at eleven, the organist appeared from a discreet side door and took her seat at the monstrous white pipe organ. At some unseen signal the congregation stood as one, golden hymnals in hand, and began to sing a familiar hymn.

Abigail breathed a sigh of relief. "Oh, I love this song," she confided to Edward. "It's one of my all-time favorites." Abigail knew many songs from memory from her years in the church choir prior to college. She didn't hesitate before joining in.

In her best choir form, she stood up straight with her arms

resting naturally at her sides, and belted out the song for all she was worth. She prided herself on her nice soprano voice, and she knew her ability to project was excellent. With the acoustics in this grand sanctuary, she had no doubt they could hear her joyful chorus all the way to Dust Bowl.

It was in the middle of the second stanza that she realized she was singing alone. Well, almost. A few parishioners made a feeble attempt to continue, but for the most part the congregation appeared to be craning their necks to see just who it was that was making all that racket. Abigail's loud singing died to a sheepish murmur in an instant.

She was deeply grateful when the interminable hymn finally ended and the congregation sat down. She dropped to her well-cushioned pew in abject humiliation. In response to Edward's questioning stare she whispered simply, "I don't know what came over me."

The arrival of the preacher saved her from further explanation. "Good morning brothers and sisters," the robed gentleman called from the glistening white pulpit. "Our topic this morning will be the importance of preserving the rain forest."

Abigail missed the rest of the sermon. Despite the preacher's skillful use of his well-trained speaking voice and dramatic gestures, she could not muster more than passing enthusiasm for the plight of poison dart frogs.

She passed the time studying the play of light through the opaque white stained glass windows on the velvety carpet below. She marveled over the massive sprays of pure white flowers that flanked the altar and spent a significant amount of time trying to count the blooms.

She had to admit it was an incredible place, much like what she imagined a cathedral should be. It was unlike anything she had ever seen, its urbane sophistication light years away from the homespun comfort of the church in Dust Bowl. Yet, something didn't seem right. It was pretty, punctual, polished. . .

❧

"So, what did you think of First Church?" Edward asked as they stood out on the front steps waiting for the crowd to dissipate. Overhead, the church bells rang out the noon hour.

"It's so—" Abigail struggled to put her ambivalent feelings into words. "Perfect."

Edward smiled his approval. "My thoughts exactly. It's perfect. First Church runs like a well-oiled machine, and that's the kind of organization I like to be associated with." He turned and gestured toward the door they had exited from. "The decor is tasteful, the services orderly, and the congregation refined—what more could you possibly ask for?"

"The sermon—"

"Was excellent, wasn't it? Frankly, I'm tired of preachers droning on about sin. It's tedious, not to mention outright offensive." He smoothed a wrinkle from the sleeve of his flawless suit. "Personally, I can't imagine God wanting to offend anyone."

"I'm not sure—"

Edward interrupted, "You know, Abigail, I've said it before, but I've got to say it again. You're good for me."

She lowered her eyes at the unexpected praise. "Thank you."

"Do you know I saw at least a half dozen business associates in church this morning? Your suggestion to attend was pure genius. Just think of the contacts I can make. That kind of association can't help but build my position in the community." He nodded sagely. "Never underestimate the importance of influential contacts."

28

It was a little after ten when Abigail slipped wearily between her sheets. She hadn't eaten supper that night. She didn't seem to have any appetite. Not likely she'd waste away. She'd eaten enough at the club's lunch buffet with Edward to hold her until morning.

She glanced over at the telephone on the nightstand. It'd be awfully nice to talk to Jarred. Maybe she should call him to report her visit to church. He'd be delighted to hear she took his suggestion. She could almost see him smile, deep dimples appearing in his bronze cheeks at the news.

She picked up the receiver and started to dial. Suddenly, she hesitated. The first thing he'd ask about would be the sermon. What Scripture had the pastor used, what did she get out of it, that sort of thing. She frowned. The pastor hadn't mentioned any Scripture at all, and she didn't think Jarred'd be too tickled to hear about the annual rainfall in the jungles of South America.

She replaced the receiver on the phone. Maybe she'd better wait and call him next week when she had something better to report.

She reached up, switched off the lamp, and lay back against her pillow in the darkness, awaiting sleep.

twenty

Abigail opened the file on the story she'd begun earlier in the day and read through what she had written.

"Now that's what I like to see," Lurline called from across the room, "dedicated *Herald* reporters hard at work after closing time."

Lurline's greeting caught her off guard and Abigail quickly swiped at her eyes with the back of her hand.

"What'cha doing, hot shot?" Lurline arrived by the side of her desk. Suddenly, she stopped and stared. "Hey, girl," she said, crouching down beside Abigail's chair. "Are you crying? What's wrong?"

"I'm not crying, exactly," Abigail sniffled. "I'm just working on a sad story."

"Sad stories are my line of work, not yours." Lurline stood up to read the writing on the screen. "Lemme see."

Annual Bridal Fair Begins Friday
This year's bridal fair, hosted by Tridico's Formal Wear and Lange's Bridal Emporium. . .

Lurline scowled down at her friend. "I think you've been working too hard, Abigail. This isn't a sad story. It's about weddings. You know, the happy union of two lovebirds. Parties, presents, tall cakes with white icing—"

"Yes, I know," Abigail said as a fat tear rolled lazily down her cheek.

Lurline looked completely bewildered. "So what are you crying about?"

Abigail shrugged, not trusting herself to speak.

Lurline sat down and studied her friend. "This is serious, isn't it?"

Abigail nodded her misery.

"Don't cry. You don't have anything to cry about. Just look at you, you've got it all."

With that, Abigail dissolved into noisy sobs.

Lurline sprang to her feet and frantically scanned the empty room for a tissue. As luck would have it, a new box sat on the desk just two cubicles away. She retrieved the box and pressed it into Abigail's hands. "There now," she said, awkwardly patting her on the shoulder, "don't cry."

"I'm okay," Abigail reassured her when the tears finally subsided. "It's nothing."

"Don't look like nothing to me," Lurline declared. She sat down again beside her friend. "Now you tell me what's wrong and I'll fix it."

Abigail gave her a watery smile. "I'm just being silly. I started to read about all those happy couples planning to get married and start their families…" Her voice faltered and new tears glistened in her eyes.

"So that's what this is all about." Lurline smacked her freckled forehead with the heel of her hand. "I don't know why I didn't think of it earlier."

Abigail dabbed her eyes with a tissue. "Think of what?"

"You keep talking about something missing from our success formula. That you feel kinda empty inside. Well, I know why! It's love, don't you see?"

"No."

"No man is an island, right?"

"I guess."

"Well, no woman is either. Here you are, wallowing in all this fine success with nobody to share it with you. You're all alone in the world—"

"I'm not exactly alone," Abigail protested. "I've got you and my family and—"

Lurline shook her head. "That's different. Family and friends are fine an' all, but what we're talking about goes much deeper. What you need is somebody to love."

"Hi, ladies!" Jarred poked his head around the corner. "Abby, I was hoping to catch you here." One look at her tear-streaked face and he was on his knees beside her in an instant. "What is it, honey?" he asked, catching her small hand in his. "What's the matter?"

Lurline shot her a warning look over the top of Jarred's head, signaling her to say nothing of their conversation. "I've got to run. My TV show comes on in thirty minutes and you know how bad traffic is at this time of night." She stood up. "Good to see you again, Jarred. Night, Abigail." She disappeared around the end of the cubicle and was gone.

Jarred's eyes searched Abigail's face. He reached up to tenderly brush a strand of hair off her cheek. "Do you want to talk about it?"

She shook her head. "I got emotional over a sad story. Silly, isn't it?" *Time to change the subject.* "What are you doing here? I didn't expect to see you in town."

He studied her another moment more before answering. "I need your help with some decisions on the house. I couldn't ask you over the phone and I didn't know when you'd be back home—so here I am." He lifted a dark brow. "You sure you're okay?"

"I'm sure," she said with a smile. It was true. She did feel okay. Funny how Jarred had that effect on her. "So what's the problem?"

"Wallpaper." Jarred made it sound like a deadly virus. "The builder's ready to order wallpaper and I don't know a thing about that kind of stuff."

He walked over to the wall of the cubicle and picked up the two heavy books he'd dropped there. He carried them back to Abigail and set them on her lap. "Can you help me?"

She chuckled at the desperation she heard in his voice. "I'd be glad to." She flipped open the cover of the first book and frowned. "I don't know, Jarred." She lifted her eyes to his. "Don't you think this is something your wife should be doing?"

Jarred froze. She watched his expression change to something serious, something unreadable. Silence stretched between them as he seemed to wrestle with some inner conflict. Finally, lips pursed with resolution, he crouched at her side. "Aw Abby, honey," he said, cradling her hand in his, "who's better suited than you?"

Abigail's heart stopped. For a split second she was confused. A strange electricity crackled in the air and it made it hard for her to think. Was he affirming her ability as a decorator or was it something more? It almost sounded like he was asking her to be his— Her eyes widened with astonishment.

Jarred licked his lips nervously. "I've gone and made a mess of things, haven't I? Let me start over. I love you, Abby. Always have." His dark eyes never left hers for an instant. "I'd be honored to have you for my wife."

All rational thought fled with his unexpected declaration of love. Abigail was incapable of speech. She simply gaped.

Jarred combed his long fingers through his hair. "I can see I've spooked you real good. I'm sorry." He stared at the floor. "I sure didn't mean for all that to slip out like it did. It's just that I've been waiting so long, and—aww, never mind."

He raised his eyes to hers. "I love you and want you to marry me. I won't press you for an answer, but I ask you to give it some thought."

"There you are, Abigail!" Edward said, suddenly appearing around the side of her cubicle. "I've been calling your apartment for half an hour. Did you forget we have a date tonight?"

The highly charged mood evaporated in a heartbeat. Abigail took a deep unsteady breath. "Hello, Edward." She closed the cover of the book and looked up at him. "No, I didn't forget our date. I was trying to finish my story before I went home." She cast a covert glance down at Jarred. "I must have lost track of time."

"No problem," he said magnanimously. Edward switched his attention to Jarred who had just gotten up off his knees. "Back again, cowboy? What is it this time? Another crisis in the continuing saga of the house building business?"

Jarred grinned. "You could say that. Seems I've got to order wallpaper in the next day or two and I came to Abby for a little advice."

Abigail was startled by the hostility she heard in Edward's voice. "There aren't any decorators in—" she offered in Jarred's defense.

"And he had no where else to turn," Edward finished irritably. "So I've heard." He looked back at Jarred. "When will this house be finished so you'll be able to give your full attention to your cows?"

Jarred seemed unperturbed by the rudeness of his question. "If everything goes according to plan, I should move in by Thanksgiving."

"You have my sincerest wishes that everything will be according to plan."

Jarred accepted his ill-concealed barb with gracious amusement. "Thank you. Since you two have plans, I won't keep you." He rested his large hand on Abigail's shoulder. "Abby, honey, I marked the ones I thought were possibilities. Look 'em over if you get a chance and I'll run in to pick up the books from you sometime this weekend. We can talk some more," he added meaningfully.

Edward stepped forward and cleared his throat. "Since you'll be back in town, perhaps you'd like to attend a little party I'm having Saturday night." He placed his hand on Abigail's other shoulder. "We'd love to have you."

If Jarred was startled by the swift change in Edward, he didn't show it. "That's real nice of you."

"Party starts at eight." Edward pulled a scrap of paper from his coat pocket and scribbled a few words on it. "Here's my address. I don't think you'll have any trouble finding the place." He handed the paper to Jarred. "The dress is black tie. That means formal, you know."

"I think I read that somewhere, but thanks for the tip." Jarred turned to wink at Abigail. "See you Saturday, honey." He touched the brim of his hat. "Goodnight."

ॐ

Abigail had just pulled the covers up under her chin when the phone rang. She fumbled in the dark for the receiver. "Hello?"

"So, what did Jarred want?" Lurline demanded without preamble.

"Hmmm? Oh, Jarred," Abigail answered distractedly. "He, uh, he wanted me to help him pick out wallpaper." She elected not to mention his marriage proposal.

"You okay, Abigail? You sound weird."

Sometimes she could swear Lurline had radar. "Not weird, just tired."

"Still fretting about that story you wrote, aren't you? Well, fret no more. I've got the solution to all your troubles."

Sensing the call would take a while, Abigail sat up and swung her legs over the side of the bed. "Oh really," she said, turning on the bedside lamp. "And what would that be?"

"You need to get married."

Abigail dropped the receiver.

"Abigail? Abigail, you there?"

Abigail scooped up the phone and gripped it tightly to her ear. "Yeah, I'm here. Sorry about that."

"No problem. So what do you think about my brainstorm? I mean about you getting married?"

"Do you have someone in mind or do I get to choose?"

"Do you get to choose?" Lurline mimicked. "What a kidder you are. Of course you get to choose. You choose Edward."

"Just like that? Doesn't he have some say in the matter?"

"Don't be obtuse, Abigail. Of course, he does. You two are perfect together. Everybody knows it. You've been seeing each other for months. It won't be long before he pops the question."

"Just suppose, for the sake of argument, that I don't want to marry Edward. Suppose that I'm in love with someone else?"

Lurline laughed. "Ridiculous. The only other guy you know is Jarred, and even if you loved him, you certainly couldn't marry him!"

Abigail was taken aback by the certainty in her friend's tone. "Why do you say that? Jarred'd make a wonderful husband."

"For somebody else, maybe, but not for you. He's from your old life. The one you've left behind. You could never go back to being the old Abigail, satisfied with the things of Dust Bowl after you've tasted real life. You'd be miserable and what's more, you'd make Jarred miserable. You both deserve better than that."

She'd make Jarred miserable. Abigail had never thought of that.

"You're different now, Abigail. You're sophisticated and worldly. Your new goals and values are light years ahead of Jarred's Dust Bowl philosophy of God and home and family. You told me so yourself."

She had a point.

"Besides, Edward is success personified. To marry him would assure you a lifetime of happiness and fulfillment. Isn't that what you want?"

Abigail lay awake long after she'd hung up with Lurline, pondering the question.

twenty-two

Abigail made a few unnecessary adjustments to the huge bouquet of fresh flowers standing atop the fine antique table in the entry hall. Edward had certainly pulled out all stops for this "little party." Over one hundred of the city's most prominent citizens had been invited to share an intimate evening at his palatial home and she had no doubt they'd all be there.

It promised to be quite a production. In addition to his regular staff, Edward had hired a squadron of uniform-clad servers to attend to the needs of the crush of elegant guests. The caterers arrived an hour ago, and already delicious smells wafted from Edward's gourmet kitchen. The florist made two trips to deliver all the fresh flower arrangements now positioned strategically throughout the house. Edward had even hired several valets.

Abigail did what she could to help, which for the most part meant staying out of the way. Until five minutes ago, when Edward excused himself to dress for the party, he had roamed the house giving commands like a five-star general. She marveled at his self-control, he was completely at ease amidst this chaos. He actually enjoyed it. It gave her a headache.

She paused in front of the huge gilded mirror to study her reflection. She stepped back and turned slowly from side to side to get the full effect. The critical appraisal was an eye-opener. While it seemed impossible, she could find no trace of Dust Bowl in the polished woman looking back at her.

Her short black dress, which only Abigail knew came from an upscale resale shop in Dallas, was simple and elegant. She'd spent the better part of an hour at the hair salon having her shoulder length, blond tresses trimmed and styled to perfection. Her flawless pink acrylic nails completed the facade. The transformation was complete.

She was the sophisticated woman of the nineties. She had it all: nice job, expensive clothes, influential friends. She'd done it; made something of herself. Something from nothing.

Abigail leaned toward the mirror for a closer look. She'd read somewhere that the eyes were the mirror of the soul. What story did her eyes tell? Did they perpetuate the lie that she was enjoying her success? Or did the blue depths betray her, proclaiming her painful emptiness for all to see?

"You look lovely," Edward said as he came to stand behind her.

She smiled at his handsome face reflected in the glass. "Thank you. So do you."

Edward accepted her compliment with a regal nod. "Thanks." He lifted his noble chin slightly. "I have my tuxedos custom made," he said as he adjusted his cuffs. "That's really the only way you can get a decent fit. You can tell a lot about a man by his formal wear."

He caught her eyes in the mirror. "I wonder if your cowboy friend will make it tonight. I don't know why," he said with a chuckle, "but I have the strangest feeling he's going to show up in a rented baby blue tux with a matching ruffled shirt. Like a rodeo clown."

Abigail swallowed hard.

While she recognized Edward's gleeful prediction was a very real possibility, it seemed disloyal to admit it. "I wouldn't worry about Jarred," she said with a manufactured smile. "He's always had a certain flair for fashion."

Edward sniffed. "Blue jeans and muddy boots do not constitute a flair for fashion. It's obvious your friendship with him has impaired your judgment." He smiled suddenly. "No matter. I believe after tonight you'll see him in a whole new light."

Abigail spun around to face Edward. "I don't understand you." Her eyes narrowed slightly. "It almost sounds like you want Jarred to show up in a baby blue tuxedo. Like you want him to make a fool of himself."

Her blunt accusation seemed to catch Edward off guard. "Maybe I do." Seeing her shocked displeasure, he stopped for a moment, carefully weighing his words.

"The man's a nuisance, Abigail," Edward huffed. "Every time I turn around, he's here. At your office, at your apartment—he always manages to have some lame excuse to stop in and see you. Frankly, I don't like it. I don't like it at all."

He frowned before adding. "I don't know, maybe I'm jealous of the guy."

Abigail was flabbergasted. "You're jealous of Jarred?"

"It sounds silly, I know." Edward shrugged in bewilderment. "What does he have that I could possibly be jealous of? I mean, the guy's a cowboy."

The doorbell chimed merrily bringing their conversation to an abrupt halt. Edward checked his reflection one last time, straightened his tie a fraction of an inch, then turned to greet his guests.

Abigail joined him, smiling and speaking mechanically while she digested this incredible bit of news. Edward was jealous? She cast a furtive glance in his direction. He often told her he found her amusing or refreshing, and several times he had commented that she was good for him, but she never considered that he might be jealous.

For the next hour her thoughts were otherwise occupied as Oklahoma's elite streamed through Edward's front door. Abigail stood by his side greeting each of the now familiar people by name.

By nine-thirty the party was in full swing with the majority of the guests clustered in the central part of the house. Conversation, food, and liquor flowed in abundance. She glanced at her watch. Where was Jarred?

"Abigail, that's the hundredth time I've seen you look at your watch in the last ten minutes. Are you going somewhere?" a woman asked.

Edward answered for her. "We've invited a childhood friend of hers to the party tonight. A cowboy." He wrapped his arm around her waist. "I think she's concerned he may have lost his way."

The woman pointed over Abigail's shoulder. "Unless I miss my guess, here comes your cowboy now."

Her announcement was accompanied by a distinct lull in the level of conversation as others noticed the new arrival. Abigail tensed, bracing herself for the worst. At least nobody was laughing. She took that as a good sign.

Slowly, calmly, she turned to face him with a bright smile pasted on her face and a heartfelt commitment to make him feel at home no matter what he was wearing.

In spite of her best intentions, she felt her mouth go slack.

Jarred was magnificent. Her heart pounded and her breath

caught in her throat as he strode across the room toward her. The crowd parted automatically in deference to his commanding presence.

He was dressed in midnight black from the top of his head to the soles of his feet. His tuxedo jacket hugged his muscular shoulders and broad chest to perfection. Even Edward would have to applaud his tailor. His crisp white shirt stood out in stark contrast to his golden bronze skin. His long legs were sheathed in what appeared to be jeans—coal black and creased like the most expensive trousers. Black boots gleamed from his feet and a black Stetson crowned his dark curls.

Abigail expelled the breath she'd been holding in a sigh. The effect of his clothing was truly dazzling, but it was his melting smile and those dimples that nearly proved her undoing. For a moment Abigail thought her legs would give way. Whether it was due to his usual effect on her senses or relief she couldn't say.

In seconds, he was at her side. "Hi, Abby, honey," he said as he bent to kiss her cheek. "Sorry I'm so late." He straightened and glanced around at the well-bred group openly gawking at the new arrival. "Your buddy sure throws a nice party."

She was too relieved to consider the goose bumps now raised on her arms. Jarred was here and that was all that mattered. She'd been so worried. Worried that he wouldn't wear the right thing, worried that he'd look foolish in front of these cultured friends. How wrong could she have been? Jarred was just perfect, wherever he was.

She leaned close to whisper, "Where in the world did you find that tuxedo?"

"What, this?" Jarred asked, plucking carelessly at the lapels. "It was hanging in my closet." In response to the blank look on her face he clarified, "It's mine."

"You own a tuxedo?"

"Beat's all, doesn't it?" he said with a laugh. "Fact is, I got tired of driving into Maxwell Flats every year to rent one. Actually," he added in an embarrassed whisper, "I don't think it was the drive that bothered me as much as the fittings. You wouldn't believe where they hang those measuring tapes and pins."

"You wear a tux once a year?"

"You didn't know this ol' country boy was so highfalutin, did you?" He laughed at her bewildered expression. "Before you get too excited I might as well confess I only do it because they make judges wear tuxes now at the Greater Dust Bowl Rodeo Finals."

She shook her head in astonishment.

"Seemed to me it would be a lot less trouble to buy one." His gaze traveled from her troubled expression to the group of people that stood by, openly watching them. He frowned uncertainly. "It looks okay, doesn't it?"

From the corner of her eye she could see several female guests practically salivating over her friend. Bless his heart, he really didn't know. "Yes, Jarred," she said with a reassuring smile as she patted his arm, "you look just fine."

His smile was back in full force. "You, too." He pushed his hat back off his forehead to give her a frank appraisal that turned her insides to mush. "You look good enough to eat."

Edward stepped in front of Abigail to extend his hand to Jarred. "Glad you could make it, Cowboy."

Jarred accepted his hand, his eyes never leaving Abigail's. "Wouldn't miss it."

Because Abigail's gaze was locked on Jarred's she missed the subtle change in Edward's expression. His eyes narrowed slightly and his perfect jaw set with steely determination.

"I have an announcement to make," Edward said coolly, "and I wanted to be sure you were here to hear it."

Abigail's eyes flew to his face. "What kind of announcement?"

He took her hand. "Come stand beside me," he said. "You're an important part of it."

Edward maneuvered the two of them to the center of the room and cleared his throat. "I wonder if I might have your attention," he called. Quiet descended over the room. Curious guests from other rooms filtered in to join the crowd. Abigail looked to Jarred and shrugged.

"I'm so glad you all could join me this evening," Edward began. "Tonight is a particularly auspicious occasion and I wanted you to share it with me."

The group watched their host expectantly.

"You've all known me long enough to know I've made it a

point not to tie myself down to one woman. Over the last few years you've seen me escort hundreds of different women and yet steadfastly shun any romantic entanglements—no matter how hard they tried."

The crowd laughed.

Edward looked down at Abigail. "Until now." He draped his arm around her waist. "Since I met Abigail several months ago at a charity function, I've become a one-woman man."

He had to speak louder to be heard over the excited murmurs. "Through that chance meeting, I have found in Abigail a soulmate, the perfect extension of myself. She's bright, witty, and possesses a wonderful sense of style. Beyond that, she and I share a common understanding of that which is truly important in life."

Edward turned to direct his statement to Abigail. "I've always prided myself on being an intelligent man, one who recognizes a good thing when he sees it. Furthermore, I didn't get where I am today by letting good things slip through my fingers." He withdrew a small square black velvet box from his jacket pocket and handed it to Abigail.

"Go ahead," he prodded, when she seemed reluctant to accept it. "Open it."

The hinged box creaked as she slowly pulled it open with trembling fingers. She stared in wide-eyed amazement at the diamond ring nestled in the velvet folds. "Edward?" she whispered.

His hands closed over hers. "I'm asking you to be my wife."

In a room where close to one hundred people gathered, you could have heard a pin drop.

Abigail stood frozen, her mind churning furiously. *Wife. Edward is asking me to be his wife.*

Jumbled thoughts raced through her head as her heart pounded madly in her chest. Though she never raised her eyes from the small parcel in her hands, she sensed the anticipation of the crowd pressing in around her. She felt each pair of eyes on her. Watching. Waiting. Panic clutched at her heart, further muddling her thoughts. She swallowed hard.

In the midst of the confusion, a single thought penetrated her befuddled mind. Edward was offering her the solution to her emptiness.

Isn't this what she wanted? Hadn't she and Lurline deter-mined that the missing element of Abigail's life was someone to share it with? Someone to love.

Someone to love. *Jarred*. Even now she could feel the power of his gaze, but she wouldn't turn to meet it. She couldn't. She knew that with a single glance her love for him would be visible to all. She couldn't allow Jarred to see it. The path she'd chosen made their love impossible. Instead of forging a life together, her commitment to success would drive them apart. She would make him miserable. And she loved Jarred too much to let that happen.

She willed her eyes to meet Edward's. He was smiling warmly at her and she managed a tremulous smile in response. Edward Winters, Oklahoma's most eligible bachelor, wanted to make her a part of his life. The man who epitomized success found her to be his soul-mate. This was almost like something out of a fairy tale. Abigail could see the headline on Sunday's society page: *Small town girl leaves rural roots behind and finds fabulous success with sophisticated millionaire.*

She studied his handsome patrician face. Edward was every-thing a girl could ever want. She knew she wasn't in love with him, but surely she could learn to love him. She'd remake her heart the way she'd remade the rest of her. Something from nothing.

"Yes, Edward," she declared resolutely. "I will marry you."

❧

Jarred stopped his truck at the foot of Blackberry Hill. Somehow he'd made the one hundred fifty mile trek from the city, though now he couldn't recall any details of the long drive.

The evening was perfectly still with not even the slightest breeze to stir the branches of the trees. His footsteps crunched in the dead grass as he climbed the hill. He moved with the labored steps of a man who'd been dealt a staggering blow.

And he had.

Hours ago he'd strolled into the society boy's fancy house a happy man. And why not? He had everything a man could ask for; he was in love with a wonderful woman and God was in His heaven.

He'd left the house in ruin.

In the span of a few minutes, Jarred had nothing. The things he held valuable became meaningless, the woman he loved committed herself to another before his very eyes, and where in the world was God?

He pushed open the door of his house and stepped inside. The light from the full moon filtered through the many windows, bathing the front hall in an eerie silver glow. The unfinished house was silent and cold.

His decision to come to Blackberry Hill was one of habit. For weeks now, he'd been coming here to dream and plan for the future. His and Abby's future.

He raised his face to the rafters and cried out his anger and frustration. "Where are You, God?"

His words evaporated into the blackness overhead. "Where are You?" he shouted again, as if daring God to show Himself.

"Why'd You let this happen? Haven't I prayed faithfully for twenty-two years for her? Weren't You listening? I wanted her for me!"

Jarred slammed his fist into the wall. "I wanted her for me!" He punched the wall again, his fist crashing through the drywall. "I trusted You all these years, and what do I get? Nothing!"

twenty-two

"Hey! You got time to look at a few pictures?"

Abigail watched in horror as her friend dropped an eighteen-inch stack of glossy magazines on her desk. "A few pictures?" she complained. "Lurline, that's got to be fifteen magazines." She picked one off the top and flipped carelessly through the pages. "I had no idea there were so many bridal magazines. It'll take a year to sort through all this." She dropped it onto the pile.

"And to answer your question," she continued irritably, "no, I don't have time. I've got an appointment to do an interview in less than an hour."

"I was only trying to help."

Abigail heard the hurt in Lurline's voice and was instantly contrite. "I'm sorry. I didn't mean to snap at you. I haven't been myself lately. I guess I've just got my mind on other things."

Lurline was grinning again. "Perfectly understandable, I mean with you planning the fairy tale wedding of the year." She dropped into the chair and propped her elbows on Abigail's desk. "Have you settled on a date yet?"

Abigail shook her head.

"I thought Edward was pressing you for a date last weekend."

"He was. And is." Abigail closed her eyes and massaged her aching temples. "He insists that we decide no later than Friday so we can reserve the church."

Lurline sighed. "Isn't that romantic? He can't wait to claim you as his bride."

"I suppose so," Abigail agreed halfheartedly. "Actually he's very concerned that if we delay too long, we'll run into scheduling conflicts with some of the season's big events. Might hurt attendance."

That bit of unromantic news did nothing to dispel Lurline's enthusiasm. "It's wonderful. Edward is rich, important, and practical." She smiled up at her friend. "What more could you ask for?"

Lurline leaned back in her chair and folded her arms across her chest. "I'll tell you, Abigail, this is all bigger than I ever imagined.

Be honest. Did you ever, in your wildest dreams, think anything like this would happen to you?"

Abigail's response was genuine. "No. Never."

&

Abigail arrived at the home of Jasper and Evelyn Revels promptly at two o'clock. As she pulled her car into the driveway, she could see the elderly couple waiting out on the porch.

"Mr. and Mrs. Revels?" she called, hurrying up the walk toward them. "I'm Abigail Bradley from the *Herald*."

Mrs. Revels reached for Abigail's hand and directed her toward the door. "Come in, won't you, dear?"

Once inside the modest home, Abigail accepted a seat on a velveteen arm chair while Jasper and Evelyn sat directly across from her on a pretty flowered couch.

"Now, dear, tell us what it is you want to know."

Abigail smiled into the eager faces leaning toward her. The couple must have been in their late seventies, yet their wrinkled countenances shone with a youthful enthusiasm Abigail rarely saw among people her own age.

"As I explained on the telephone, I'd like to feature you two in my upcoming column. Since you will be celebrating your fiftieth wedding anniversary on Saturday, I wanted to ask you what is your secret to reaching such a milestone. I believe our readers would appreciate any words of wisdom you can share."

The couple exchanged a quick loving glance. Jasper spoke first. "Ain't no secret, really. When we got married fifty years ago we decided it was gonna be forever."

"So you made a commitment to the relationship."

Jasper stroked his chin as he considered the word. "Yes, indeed, that's exactly what we did." He laughed. "We promised to love each other until the day we died, even if it killed us."

Evelyn giggled at her husband's choice of words. She slid her hand into his, the aged ebony fingers interlocking. "Sometimes it was hard," she admitted. "There were a few times when keeping things together nearly did kill us, but by the grace of God, we did it."

Abigail was scribbling furiously in her notepad. "So we have commitment." She ticked commitment off her own mental list.

Edward thought she was good for him and wanted to make her a permanent part of his life. That sounded like commitment.

"What other ingredients do you think helped keep you together all these years?"

Jasper shrugged. "We laugh a lot."

Evelyn nodded. "That's the truth. I s'pect anybody thinking about marriage better have a fine sense of humor. Seems like a little laughter smoothes out a whole world of troubles. What does the Bible say? 'A merry heart doeth good like a medicine'?"

Abigail wrote "a sense of humor" under "commitment." She and Edward were okay there. He thought she was a riot.

"Better add forgiveness to that paper, young lady. Folks can't make a marriage last if they aren't able to forgive mistakes and let 'em go."

Evelyn nodded her approval and Abigail added "forgiveness" to the list. She didn't know whether she could add that to her personal list. She was too careful around Edward to make any mistakes for him to forgive.

"What about common goals and similar interests?" Abigail asked. She knew she and Edward had those in abundance. Success, success, success.

"I don't know about similar interests, dear. But now similar values—I'd say Jasper and I see eye to eye on what's truly important."

"It don't hurt that I'm married to the prettiest woman ever was." Jasper winked at his wife.

"Jasper's always flirting that way with me." Evelyn was clearly delighted. "Can you imagine him saying things like that about me after all these years?"

Abigail grinned. She could see that Jasper's words were not empty compliments meant to impress a visiting newspaper reporter. There was a familiar glimmer in his dark eyes—seemed like she'd seen one like it somewhere before—one that spoke volumes about his appreciation of his wife. "I'll add physical attraction to the list."

Evelyn leaned forward to confide. "Do you know I still get goose bumps when he kisses me?"

Abigail's fingers went slack and her pen rolled onto the floor.

Goose bumps? Jarred's face came to mind and with it a clear recollection of where she'd seen that glimmer before. *Jarred!* He looked at her just that way.

Abigail jerked her attention back to the interview. Jasper and Evelyn appeared to be conferring about something. Abigail bent to retrieve her pen. "Is there anything else you'd like to mention?"

"Seems like it wouldn't be right if we didn't give credit where credit is due. Fact is, God has blessed us."

Abigail was focused again. "You've mentioned God several times. Are you religious people?"

"If you mean by religious, do we love God with all our hearts and look expectantly to His son Jesus for our salvation, then, yes ma'am, we are religious."

Abigail scratched out a few notes then paused to look up at Evelyn, her pen poised to write again. "Do you think your faith in God has had anything to do with the success of your relationship?"

Both people answered at the same time.

"Certainly."

"No doubt."

"I wonder if you would clarify that. For my readers."

Jasper looked to Evelyn and nodded for her to speak. "God is the glue that holds our marriage together. His power and presence make it possible for us to do those things you've been writing on that list. Heaven knows none of those things come naturally to humans."

Evelyn leaned over to study Abigail's notebook. "Take commitment, for starters," she said, pointing to the top word. "By following God's own example to us we are able to stick it out together—whatever the circumstances. He doesn't ever give up on us and His faithfulness teaches us how to be faithful."

Abigail wasn't writing anymore. Her eyes were trained on Evelyn, her ears claiming every word.

"Our sense of humor, even in hard times, is a product of our hope in God. We know He's taking care of us, and doing the very best thing for us and that knowledge is enough to make a body downright giddy."

"I can see the part about forgiveness being tied to your faith," Abigail said. "After all, Christianity is all about forgiveness, isn't it?"

Evelyn grinned. "Yes, dear, it is. We are all mighty big sinners, yet God forgives us. Can we do any less for the people we love?"

"What's next on the list?" Jasper wanted to know.

"Values."

"That's simple enough. Our values come straight from the Bible. If they're good enough for God, they're good enough for us."

"But the Bible is so old—"

"Yes, it is, dear," Evelyn agreed. "Old and enduring. The truths written there have passed the test of time. What a comfort that is."

Jasper was nodding enthusiastically, obviously enjoying himself. "What's next?"

"Physical attraction."

"Amen!"

"Now Jasper," Evelyn scolded him with a reluctant grin. "You'd better let me take that one." She leaned toward Abigail. "You're probably wondering what two old folks know about physical attraction."

Jasper snorted, and Evelyn squeezed his hand to silence him.

"That attraction to one another—that's God's gift to His children. I even think He gives us special sight, the ability to see past the outward form to the heart of the one we love. And you gotta figure He's a powerful God that He's able to help Jasper see past all these wrinkles and gray hair."

Jasper kissed his wife on the cheek and Abigail laughed. "That wraps up my questions for you. Thank you so much for your time."

She tucked her pen into the notebook and closed it. "I wonder, it's a bit off the subject, but may I ask you one more question? Do you ever feel like life is one big treadmill?"

"Heavens no!" Evelyn grinned. "Life is an adventure, thanks to our loving God."

"I hope you won't think I'm prying, but don't I see a shiny diamond on your finger?" Jasper asked. "Does that mean you're about to marry?"

Abigail nodded.

"That's wonderful," Evelyn said with a warm smile. "I'm sure he's a lovely young man and you'll be as happy as Jasper and I have been."

Abigail stood up to leave. "I'm beginning to wonder."

⤫

It was early, before seven, and the office was deserted when Abigail began to look over the notes from yesterday's interview with Jasper and Evelyn. A smile pulled at the corner of her mouth as she scanned the pages. Talk about a marriage made in heaven.

Thoughts of her impending marriage surfaced. Her union with Edward was the sum total of all her highest aspirations. There was no denying they made an impressively successful pair. And yet, did they truly fit any of the criteria the Revels had outlined for her in the interview? And if not, did it matter?

Somehow she knew it did. Tying oneself for life to another was pretty serious business. Suddenly, she knew why she hadn't been able to set a wedding date. She was scared.

She couldn't dismiss these doubts as a bout of normal pre-marital jitters. She knew it went deeper. She was truly afraid she was making a mistake.

How could she know? The stack of bridal magazines on her desk caught her eye. She sincerely doubted there was one time-tested truth in the whole mess of them. She needed someone to talk to. Someone whose wisdom she could rely on.

Her first impulse was to call Jarred. Then she remembered how he had disappeared after she said yes to Edward. The thought brought a heavy sense of loss to her heart.

A second choice filtered into her mind. Her dad. Hadn't she always looked to him as a source of wisdom and counsel? Never mind that she'd scorned his advice over the last few years. She knew without a doubt he could help.

By seven-twenty she had typed a message for her supervisor explaining that she had some urgent personal business to take care of this morning, dropped the note and the first draft of her story in his message slot, and was headed for Dust Bowl.

She pulled up in her parents' driveway a little before ten. Her heart sank. Their car wasn't there. That's what she got for being so impulsive and driving all the way home without calling and checking first.

Deeply disappointed, Abigail turned the key in the ignition and the motor sprang to life. With a heavy sigh she shifted the car into reverse. As she turned to back down the driveway she thought she heard someone call her name. She swung around to see her father running from around the side of the house toward her car.

"Abby, girl! What are you doing home? Everything all right?"

She'd had the whole trip home to rehearse exactly what she wanted to say to her dad. After several minutes of chitchat she would subtly direct the course of the conversation toward her upcoming nuptials, and casually seek his input. No big deal.

One look at the concern on his beloved weathered face, and her reserve went right out the window. "Daddy," she cried, hot tears coursing down her cheeks. "Oh, Daddy."

The door was open and she was enveloped in his comforting embrace in the blink of an eye. Safe in his strong arms, she cried harder.

"Abby, girl," he said as the flood of tears tapered off. "I don't think I've seen you cry like this since you were a little girl." He wrapped his arm around her shoulder and led her into the house. "Come inside and tell me all about it."

Once he'd settled her on the couch, he disappeared down the hall. Seconds later he reappeared. "Here now," he said, pressing a cool damp washcloth into her hand. "Wipe your face and then we can talk."

Abigail smiled in spite of herself. In her family, a cool damp washcloth was the beginning of the healing process. No matter the ailment, be it temper tantrum, hurt finger, or broken heart, the remedy was the same. Wipe your face.

She did as she was told. Miraculously, as it had in times past, the cool cloth brought comfort and a sense of quiet to her mind. How could she have ever doubted his wisdom?

"Now then," he said with a chuckle. "I take it this isn't just a social call."

She shook her head.

"Your mother is at her Ladies' Guild Meeting this morning.

She'll be home around noon if you want to wait and talk with her."

"Actually, I came home to talk with you. I need your advice."

He looked pleased as he stroked his whiskered chin. "You came to the right place. You know how your old dad likes to spout off advice."

She reached over to squeeze his hand. "I'm counting on it."

Samuel waited a full three minutes for his daughter's explanation. When none was forthcoming he prodded gently, "How's things at the newspaper?"

"Fine."

That narrowed things down a bit. "How's that young man of yours? What's his name?"

"Edward. He's fine."

"Hmmmm," Samuel said, rubbing his fingers across his mouth. "So, honey," he asked after another extended pause, "If everything is fine, then what were all the tears about?"

As she raised her eyes to his, she felt her own fill with moisture. "Everything's fine," she said in a tiny voice. "Everything except me."

Her confession reopened the floodgate of tears. Samuel sat beside her on the couch and held her in his arms, rocking her gently.

"I'm sorry," she hiccuped, swiping ineffectually at her eyes with the back of her hand. "I don't know what's the matter with me. I ought to be the happiest person in the world." She sniffed loudly. "I've got a great job, beautiful clothes, and influential friends. I've got Oklahoma's most eligible bachelor waiting to marry me just as soon as I set the date." A tear rolled down her cheek. "All that, and I'm miserable."

Her father nodded sagely. "Stands to reason."

Her head snapped up. "I'm sorry?"

"Those are all fine things, you understand. There's nothing wrong with having nice things and doing what you like, but if it's satisfaction and purpose you're looking for, you're barking up the wrong tree."

She was beginning to regret her impulse to come home. "I'm not sure you understand—"

"I understand perfectly." He smiled kindly into his daughter's eyes. "Honey, you're caught in a trap that is as old as time. You're in good company though. Why, even old King Solomon tried to find satisfaction in those kinds of things. Couldn't find it, though. Neither will you."

He chucked her under the chin. "Now don't look so down-hearted. If you've got to make mistakes, might as well make them while you're young and can learn from them. There's still time to fix them. We've just got to get you back to the basics."

"Like what?"

"Jesus."

She shook her head. "No good. I've already tried religion. I've been going to church regularly and it hasn't helped a bit."

"Now, Abby girl, I'm not talking about religion. I'm talking about Jesus. You spending much time with Him lately?"

It probably wouldn't count that she said grace every night before dinner. "Well, no. Not really."

"I didn't think so. Now I'm gonna let you in on a little secret."

Abigail leaned forward to catch his whispered words. "There isn't any true peace, fulfillment, or purpose in life without Jesus. None at all. Let me tell you what Jesus says in the Bible. He says, 'I came that you might have life. . .abundant life.'" He turned to his daughter. "Isn't that what you're looking for?"

"I don't know, am I?"

"Well, sure you are. It goes by a different name now, like fulfillment or success, but it all means the same thing. It's peace and satisfaction deep down inside that says, 'I'm content. My life counts for something. I see purpose in my existence.'"

"It does sound good," Abigail admitted.

"You bet it does. Man struggles all his life to come to that place. 'Course, he doesn't have to. He could just go to God." He squeezed Abigail's hand. "Funny how we miss the things that are the most obvious."

"I'll admit it. I'm slow to catch on. But I'm desperate. I'll go back to the basics. Just tell me what to do."

"Go home and read your Bible. Start with the book of John, a chapter a day. Pray. Once you've finished your reading, talk to Jesus about it. Ask Him what He wants you to get out of it. Get to know Him, Abby. It'll change your life."

"I'd like that."

"Figured you would." Samuel glanced at his watch. "Mother'll be home in half an hour and we're heading up to Audrey's for some lunch. Can you join us?"

Abigail grinned. It was obvious the conversation was over. Her father believed the problem solved. It didn't make much sense that such a simple thing could remedy her problems, but something much deeper than common sense urged her to try it. "I better not," she said in answer to his question. "I've got to get back to the office and finish up the story I'm working on."

Her father walked her to the car, his arm draped around her waist. "Thanks, Dad." She kissed him on the cheek before climbing into the car and fastening her seatbelt. A question that weighed heavily on her heart sprang to her lips. "Have you heard from Jarred recently?"

Her father's face grew grim. "Not too much since he picked up those wallpaper books you left for him. Hasn't been himself lately."

"It's all my fault, you know. I didn't mean to hurt him—"

"I know you didn't, honey. And I don't want you to fret about ol' Jarred. He'll come through this right as rain. Some things take time. If you think about him, you might say a prayer for him. I know it'd mean a great deal."

Now that was a twist. Jarred'd been praying for her and her silly requests for years. Never once had she offered to pray on his behalf. "I'll do it. I mean it. I'll pray really hard for him."

Her father patted her arm. "I know you will. Say, when are we gonna meet your fella? Seems like a mother and father ought to get to know their future son-in-law."

"I don't know. He's so busy," she hedged. She looked away to offer a little white lie. "He's anxious to meet you and Mom."

"You've met his parents, I'm sure. What are they like?"

"Actually, I haven't met them. Yet. Edward's not close with his family. There's no problem or anything," she added quickly, "they just don't keep in touch. He's very busy with work. Have I mentioned he owns a huge company? Built it from the ground up. He's a self-made man, Dad."

"I bet that comes as a real surprise to God." He dismissed the topic with a good-natured chuckle. "I'm glad you came by today. I've missed our talks. You won't forget what I told you now, will you? Read your Bible, and get to know your Lord. I guarantee, it'll change your life."

Abigail felt a surge of unadulterated optimism as she backed down the driveway. Somehow she knew her father was right.

twenty-three

"Hey, buddy! Long time no see."

"Been busy. Fill it up, will you?"

Phillip took the gruff answer in stride. "Be glad to." He stuck the nozzle into the gas tank of the truck and lifted the lever on the rusty pump.

"So," he said appearing back at the window, "what is it that's keeping you so busy you haven't got time to come to church or visit with your oldest friend? And don't bother to tell me it's 'cause you're moving into the house. I know better than that."

Something flashed in Jarred's dark eyes. "Sounds like you've got it all figured out. Why don't you tell me?" he growled in annoyance.

Phillip braced both hands on the roof of the pickup truck and leaned slightly forward to meet his friend at eye level. "I'd say you're hurting pretty bad and you've crawled off with your tail between your legs to lick your wounds."

Jarred's hands clenched the steering wheel. "Let me warn you, my oldest friend, my mood's black enough right now that I'd enjoy a good fight."

"Come on then," Phillip invited cheerfully. "Come out here and hit me." He swung open Jarred's door. "Anything's better than watching you mope yourself to death."

Jarred climbed out and stood face to face with the man he'd called friend since he could first say the word. After sizing him up for a moment he shoved his fists in his pockets and said, "It's no use. As much as I'd like to wipe that smug grin off your face, I can't hit you. Your momma would take it out of my hide."

Phillip laughed. "Thank heavens for Momma!" He wrapped his arm around Jarred's shoulders and led him toward the station. "Since you're out of the truck now, why don't you come in and have a cup of coffee with me?"

"Do I have a choice?"

"None."

Inside, Phillip poured both men a cup of steaming coffee. For a moment they drank in silence.

"Look, Jarred, about my sister—"

"I don't want to talk about it."

Phillip would not be deterred. "I know this thing with Abby must have come as a real shock to you—"

"Shock doesn't do justice to what I feel. Try rage. Betrayal."

"Well she deserves all that and more. After all—"

"I'm not angry with Abby." Jarred's expression softened. "She's not to blame. She can't help it if she's not in love with me. Old Edward is a pretty smooth guy. Rich, handsome, worldly. No, I don't blame her for choosing a guy like that over a hick like me. I place all the blame at the feet of God."

"God?"

"Look, Phillip, I don't want to talk about it."

"I don't get it. Why's God to blame? What's He got to do with it?"

"Everything and nothing," Jarred spat out the words. "He made her everything I could ever want. I've prayed every day for twenty-two years for her. First, that she'd grow into the woman He called her to be and second, that she would be mine. His answer is to give me nothing."

"I'm sorry."

Jarred whirled on his friend. "I was faithful! I prayed and I trusted God to take care of everything. I never doubted Him for a minute. And what do I get? Nothing."

"I get it. You don't get your own way, so you're mad at God."

"You don't get anything!"

"Wait just a minute. Did God ever promise Abby to you? Where is it written that you should get everything you want?"

"Nowhere, it's just—"

"But you figured since you prayed hard for twenty-two years that it entitles you to her. Is that right?"

"No, it's not right. You're deliberately misunderstanding me."

"Face it, Jarred. What it all boils down to is you didn't get what you want from God, and now you're angry."

"That's oversimplifying things a bit."

"Maybe so. But truth is truth. Don't get me wrong, Jarred. I wanted it to be you and Abby. I know the folks feel the same way. We're sick about this Edward fella. We're praying hard for Abby to see the light. But the issue here is your relationship with God.

Nothing is more important than that."

"Look," Jarred slammed his empty coffee cup on the counter. "I don't want to talk about it."

Phillip stepped into his path. "You probably don't, but you're going to anyway."

Jarred's dark brow climbed ominously.

"You're like a brother to me. I've admired you all my life. You've always been the strong one, the rock. I don't know how many times your faith has helped carry me through some rough spots. And I can't believe a faith that strong is washed up because you didn't get your own way. Strikes me that faith like that is no faith at all."

Jarred suddenly looked weary. "I love her, Phillip." He headed out the door.

"But what about God?" Phillip called after him. "What about your commitment to Him? Can you throw it away because His plan isn't yours?" He moved into the doorway, shouting to be heard above Jarred's engine, "Or can you say as Job, 'Though He slay me, yet will I hope in Him'?"

&

Abigail stepped off the elevator at the ground level balancing two steaming cups of coffee on a stack of magazines. She followed the sound of voices past the storage rooms to the only inhabited offices on the floor. Obituaries.

Beyond the front desk and over the top of the partition, she could see Lurline's orange curls bobbing furiously as she worked at her terminal. Abigail slipped unnoticed around the corner and took the empty chair in the back of her cubicle.

"Good morning," she sang out cheerfully. "Got time for a break?"

"EEEEEEEEEEE!" Lurline squealed as she clapped a bony hand over her heart. "Abigail Bradley, you 'bout scared me to death." She recovered with a wide grin. "Of course, if I was gonna drop over dead, seems like I couldn't pick a finer place than Obituaries." She mulled over the concept for a moment. "I bet I'd get a real fine write-up. Might even throw in a picture." She posed with a horrible grimace. "What d'ya think?"

"Gruesome," Abigail said with a shake of her head. "Hopelessly gruesome."

Lurline cackled with delight.

"I brought you a cup of coffee."

"Mmmm. Thanks." She accepted one of the cups and drank deeply. "So what brings you to the catacombs? We aren't usually honored with the presence of a top-rated reporter."

"I came to return these magazines to you," she said, nodding toward the stack, "and to tell you we were wrong."

Lurline took the magazines and dropped them on the floor. "Wrong? What are you talking about?"

"We were wrong. About everything."

"You better back up. I missed something here."

"I've been doing a lot of thinking over the past few weeks, about a lot of different things."

"Now I'm worried. Your thinking always leads to trouble."

"I'm serious, Lurline. Since I've known you, we've made it our goal to make something of ourselves. We've read hundreds of magazines and followed the advice of experts to the letter to find success. We've bought the right clothes, met the right people, targeted the right positions, all with the intention of remaking ourselves and finding success."

"That's right," Lurline said proudly. "We have. And you've done it. Just look at you. You're the picture of success."

"I thought so, too. But we were wrong."

"You keep saying that."

"The reason why we were wrong is because from the very beginning, we've been mistaken about what true success is. Our definition was faulty."

Lurline shook her head. "I don't see how that can be. I mean, it's not like we made it up. You said it yourself. We got it from the experts."

"Yes, but we made one critical mistake. We forgot the first rule of reporting."

"Bad news sells?"

Abigail couldn't resist a grin. "No, silly. It's check your sources. Our so-called experts aren't experts at all. They're just people whose opinions are in favor at the time. When the tide of public opinion changes, they'll change their 'absolutes' to fit the latest pattern of correct. Their only wisdom is how to say stuff that'll sell magazines."

"Well sure, that's true," Lurline said with a shrug. "But I don't see the problem."

"The problem is that our foundation is shaky. Worse than that, it has holes. My admittedly limited experience with success tells me it doesn't satisfy. There's not a prestigious enough job, not enough designer clothes, not a relationship on earth that'll fill up this terrible little void inside. It's clear that no amount of our success will swallow up this feeling of emptiness—the constant question of: 'Is this all there is?' "

"Terrific. Now I'm totally depressed. So where does that leave us?"

"Back at the beginning. What we need is a new definition of success."

"And where will we find this new definition, may I ask?"

Abigail smiled. "From the Bible."

Lurline's eyes widened in horror. "Uh-oh. I can see the deadlines are getting to you. You're starting to crack under the pressure of work. Maybe Robinson can give you some time off."

"I'm serious, Lurline. What could be a better place than the Bible to get tried and true answers to life's questions?"

"So what you're telling me is you're gonna get religious."

"Heavens no! This has nothing to do with religion. I'm talking about a relationship with Jesus Christ."

Lurline rolled her eyes. "Why is it that fails to comfort me?"

"That's okay. I wasn't convinced myself until I took a look at it. I'm telling you, this is what we've been missing. Do you know what Jesus says? 'I came that they might have life, and might have it abundantly.'"

"Abundance is good."

Abigail ignored her. "By abundant life He means life with meaning—one overflowing with peace, contentment, and satisfaction. True success! He is telling us He is the foundation for true success."

Lurline waved her hand. "No offense here but how do we know this is better than the advice we get from magazines. I mean, at least they're current."

"For fashion news we need current. For direction in life we need timeless. Don't you see? The fact that the Bible is old is actually a plus. Its truths don't change with the tide of public opinion. They're eternal. And they're from God. Talk about your reliable sources."

Lurline rubbed her chin between her thumb and forefinger. "I never thought about it like that before."

Abigail heard her defenses lower. "We are God's creation. Who knows better than He what we need to be fulfilled?"

She moved her chair closer to Lurline's. "It's not my place to choose how you define success. But I know you've placed your faith in me to find it for both of us. I've finally found it. And I want you to know.

"Back home you got a firsthand taste of just how hopeless life can be. What did you say one time? 'Life was a meaningless treadmill.' You were right. It is. Even here in the city with all the nice trappings of job and clothes and social prominence, it's still a meaningless treadmill. Unless you have Jesus."

For a moment the women sat in silence. Lurline's freckled brow was furrowed in concentration. Finally Lurline asked softly, "Okay, so how do we get off the treadmill?"

Abigail pulled her into a quick hug. "It's so easy. We ask Jesus to be the Lord of our lives—to give us meaning and purpose."

"You first."

"Somehow I knew you'd say that." Abigail grinned. "I already have. Actually, I did it when I was ten years old and first realized I was a sinner and needed a Savior. The pastor talked about it in church one Sunday. He told us Jesus died on the cross to pay the price for my sins. I believed it and I accepted Him then. But while I made Him my Savior, I didn't make Him my Lord. I didn't want Him to be in charge. I figured I knew better than He what I wanted. Unfortunately, I was wrong.

"Anyway, after I got back into my Bible a couple of weeks ago, really reading it, I discovered what I had done. Jesus must be Savior and Lord for me to live the abundant life. I apologized to God and asked Him to forgive me for being such an idiot. Then I asked Him to give me another chance."

"Think He'll do it?"

"I know He will," Abigail declared. "Not only will He forgive me, but He will actually help me to make Jesus my Lord. It's a win-win situation."

Lurline was all smiles. "I've always been a big proponent of win-win. So, uh—how do I do it?"

"I'll pray with you, if you like. I'll say the words, and you can repeat them after me." Her expression became serious. "But I want this to be your idea, not mine. It's got to be a true commitment from the heart. Your heart."

Lurline nodded. "It will be."

Abigail took Lurline's hand and they bowed their heads. "Father, I am a sinner. I deserve to be punished. I know that You sent Your son, Jesus, to die on the cross to take the punishment for my sins. I gladly accept His sacrifice on my behalf. I accept Jesus as my Savior. But I want to do more than that, I want to make Jesus my Lord. I want Him to run my life. Please give me the strength to yield to His direction. Thank you for loving me and hearing my prayer. Amen."

Abigail squeezed Lurline's hand as she repeated the Amen. "It's done. You've started a brand new life."

Lurline looked at her arms. Goose bumps. Tears glistened in her eyes as she quipped. "Finding life in Obituaries. Imagine that." She raised earnest eyes to Abigail. "So, where do we go from here?"

"Good question. First, we get to know God better. You'll want to fit a little Bible reading into your schedule, somewhere between *Ladies First Magazine* and *Extravagance Digest*. Then, we need to find a church. We need a place where they preach from the Bible. I've heard about a small church at the corner of Madison and Sixteenth. I have an idea it's just what we need."

"What about our jobs? Do you think it's a problem we want to earn money and get ahead? Is wanting success bad?"

"Not at all. Mind you, I'm no Bible scholar, but my understanding is that jobs are fine. Whether we are homemakers or corporate CEOs, the key is perspective. Our satisfaction and purpose in life come through Jesus. He alone can fulfill us. All the rest is details."

"This is so cool. I mean it, we are on to something big here." She paused. "Say, what does Edward say about all this?"

"He hasn't heard. Yet."

twenty-four

Jarred arrived at the sanctuary thirty minutes before the service. The room was dark and cool and smelled of history. Not the musty dank smell of decay, but an aromatic blend of wood and wax that testified to years of loving service to the Father. Jarred breathed deeply.

The fading sunlight of late afternoon lit the stained glass windows over the altar with an golden glow. Drawn toward the light, Jarred labored slowly up the aisle, his broad shoulders bent as though weighed down with heavy burdens. He came to a halt before the carved oak altar and knelt there, leaning his elbows on the worn railing and burying his face in his hands.

"Father, I am so unworthy to be called Your child. How could I boast about my faithfulness? My feeble attempts at devotion are nothing in the light of Your faithfulness. I've been so wrapped up in bitterness and selfish pride that I have failed to see Your great love and mercy. Forgive me."

Jarred didn't know how long he'd been praying there when he felt a firm hand on his shoulder.

"Jarred, my friend," Pastor Johnson greeted him in a gently hushed tone. "Will I be disturbing you if I turn on the lights? Service will be starting in a few minutes."

Jarred raised a smile to the older man. "Not at all, Pastor. I'm finished here."

"I can see by the look on your face that you and the Father have worked out your differences. I'm glad of it. It's misery to be at odds with Him."

"You think I'll ever get smart enough to realize it's God's way or no way?"

Pastor Johnson chuckled. "If you ever do, you can give me lessons!"

"Hey, Pastor! Jarred! What's going on? Did I miss a meeting here?" Phillip called from the back of the sanctuary.

Jarred strode down the aisle to meet his friend. Phillip eyed him suspiciously.

"Looking a little nervous there," Jarred observed wryly. "'Fraid

I'm going to bite your head off?"

Phillip shrugged. "Something like that."

Jarred reached out and clapped him on the back. "No need to worry. I'm not angry with you. Fact is, I'm beholden to you. You said some hard things to me the other day. Things I needed to hear. I'm glad you're friend enough to say them."

Phillip's quick smile spread from ear to ear. "I'm glad to hear that." He clasped Jarred's hand in his and pumped enthusiastically. "Real glad. Say, you're coming to dinner, aren't you? Mom's putting out quite a spread this Thanksgiving. There's enough food there to feed an army."

"I'll be there. Gotta run home quick after the service and change clothes. I came here straight from the barn. Seems I had some pretty urgent business to attend to."

"I'm glad to hear that, friend. Mighty glad."

❧

Jarred passed quickly through his darkened house into the master bathroom where he turned on the shower. It took him a minute or two to locate the box with towels in it. He'd been moved in a week already, but he just wasn't in a hurry to unpack. Somehow, the house didn't seem like home.

He berated himself for being so dismal as he stepped under the stream of hot water. *Look at the bright side. Things can only get better.*

After his time in prayer at church this afternoon he could say that with conviction. Things would get better.

He had no doubt with time his grief would lessen. The ever present heaviness in his chest would be replaced with a dull ache. No point in kidding himself. He'd always love Abby. After twenty-two years, it had become a habit. But he'd get through this. All things were possible with God.

He'd dried off and pulled on clean jeans when he heard the door chime. He grabbed a denim shirt from the closet and was buttoning it up when he opened the front door.

"Hi, Jarred."

A fresh spike of pain drove through his heart. "Abby?"

She watched him expectantly for a few seconds, waiting for him to invite her in, but when no invitation seemed forthcoming she asked, "Mind if I come in?"

"Come in?" he repeated blankly. "Yeah, sure. Come in." He stepped out on the porch and looked from side to side. Seeing no one, he turned back to Abby to ask, "Where's your buddy?"

"I'm alone."

"Oh." It seemed to take forever for the information to get to his brain. She looked so good, he couldn't stop staring. He shook his head to clear it. "I didn't expect to see you today. I mean, your mother didn't mention you'd be home."

"It was a surprise." Abigail grinned up at him. "Do you need to dry off? I can wait."

"Dry off?" It dawned on him that rivulets of cold water were dripping from his wet hair down his face and neck and onto his shirt. He laughed uncertainly. "Yeah, I need to. I'll be right back."

He sprinted down the hall to the bathroom, tore off his now soaked shirt, and tossed it on the floor. He yanked another towel from the box.

"The house looks great!" Abigail called down the hallway.

"Thanks," he called back as he ruffled the towel through his wet hair. He had to bite his tongue to keep from telling her the looks improved a hundred times the minute she stepped in the door. He fought the urge to tell her that she belonged here with him—in the house he built for her.

He could hear Abigail walking across the hardwood floors. "Hey," he heard the smile in her voice, "I see you took my advice on the wallpaper. Smart move."

Jarred said nothing. It would be best if he didn't confess he'd gotten so weird that he actually cherished each inch of paper as though it somehow brought a part of her into his life. He picked up a brush and dragged it through his hair.

"I came over tonight because I wanted to offer you a little more advice."

He reached into the closet and grabbed another shirt off the hanger. "Shoot."

"I think you should marry me."

Jarred's arm missed the sleeve. Twice.

He finally jammed his arms into the shirt as he stepped into the hall. Abigail was waiting just five feet away, her blue eyes dancing, her face wreathed in smiles.

"I'm sorry," Jarred began, "I—what did you say?"

Abigail took a step closer. "I said I think you ought to marry me. Really. I'd make a nice addition to the place."

Jarred was dumbstruck. "But—"

She closed the distance between them. "I love you, Jarred. I have all my life." She pulled his forgotten shirt closed and began to button it for him. "I've been a bit confused. I thought I had to give up everything dear to me and remake myself into someone else so I could be a success."

She looked up into his face. "I was wrong. And miserable. It took me a while to figure out I had everything I'd ever want or need all the time. I love you so much. Can you forgive me?"

Jarred continued to stare in silence.

Abigail put her hands on her hips. "I can see that I've dazzled you with my city girl brilliance, so I'm gonna ask you again, real slow." She took his hands in hers and gazed up into his eyes. "Jarred Worth, will you marry me?"

With a whoop, Jarred pulled her into his arms and kissed her soundly. When their lips finally parted, Abigail leaned her head against his chest and whispered breathlessly, "I'll take that as a yes."

twenty-five

"While you girls are putting on your makeup, I'm going out to the sanctuary to see if I can help Irma with the decorations. Abby, I'll be back in ten minutes to help you with your dress." Lottie Bradley pressed a quick kiss on her daughter's cheek before ducking out of the small Sunday school room they'd converted to a bride's room.

"Hey, while we've got a minute alone, there's something I've been wanting to ask you," Lurline said.

Abigail put the finishing touches on Lurline's mascara, then straightened. "Yes?"

"I know this is probably a tacky time to ask, what with you getting married in less than half an hour, but what exactly happened between you and Edward? Last thing I knew, you were happily engaged and headed off to tell him about Jesus."

"Correction. Miserably engaged."

"I didn't know you were miserable."

Abigail sat on the folding metal chair across from her friend. "I was, but I didn't know why until I started reading my Bible. It didn't take long to see that I was doing everything, even selecting the man I would spend the rest of my life with, for all the wrong reasons. That day when I came down to your office to tell you what I had discovered, I had already decided to call off the wedding."

"How'd he take it?"

Abigail laughed. "Extremely well. So well I probably should have been offended. After I told him everything, he complimented me on my ability to rationally evaluate the long range potential of our relationship, and thanked me for breaking up soon enough for him to cut his losses."

Lurline groaned. "That man hasn't got an ounce of romance in his entire body. So that was the end, huh?"

"No. I couldn't let him go until I told him what I found. I told him about my struggle to find meaning and fulfillment. I explained to him that in Jesus Christ I found the source of the abundant life I've been looking for. And I explained it was available to him as well. But he wasn't interested."

"Not interested in fulfillment?"

Abigail shook her head. "He said it was fine for me, but he didn't need it. He felt it might dull his business instincts and he couldn't risk losing that competitive edge."

"You know, for a smart man, he's not too bright."

"He hasn't got the corner on stupidity, that's for sure. Here I was, planning to marry a man I didn't love, because of his wealth and social connections." She shook her head ruefully. "Imagine believing marriage to anyone would make me successful and fulfilled."

"I'm afraid I'm partially to blame. After all, going after Edward was my idea, not yours."

Abigail picked up the pot of blush and bent to apply a light pink streak to Lurline's freckled cheeks. "We had such big plans, didn't we? A couple of country yokels gonna remake ourselves and take the world by storm." She smiled down at her friend. "It's taken me an awfully long time to figure out that only God can make something from nothing."

The door swung open and her mother swept into the room. "Oh, Abby, Mrs. Griggs has outdone herself. The church is positively beautiful. Candles, flowers, ribbons—it's all so romantic." She pulled a tissue from the pocket of her gown and dabbed her eyes. "Mercy, I don't have time for this now. We've got to get you girls dressed."

They helped Lurline into her gown first. Lottie lowered the emerald green velvet over her head and adjusted it over her shoulders and waist while Abigail pulled the zipper up in back.

Lurline caught a glimpse of herself in the full length mirror propped against the wall. "My first long dress," she said, swishing the full skirt from side to side.

"You look lovely," Lottie said fondly.

"I do, don't I?" Lurline cocked her head to one side and grinned at her reflection. "Positively stylish. I can't wait for Suzanne to see me. It'll kill her." Having uttered her gleefully morbid prediction, she swung around to face Abigail. "We'd better get the future Mrs. Worth dressed or she'll have to get married in her jeans."

Abigail obediently dressed in her slip and shoes while her mother and Lurline gently lifted her wedding gown from its hanging bag. They carefully lowered the yards of shimmering white satin over Abigail's head so as not to ruin the upswept hairstyle she wore for her wedding. She stood still while her mother fastened the long row of tiny pearl buttons up her back and Lurline tackled the buttons on her long fitted sleeves.

When Lottie was satisfied everything was in order, she pulled Abigail's veil from its box and secured the long expanse of filmy white tulle to Abigail's hair with a jeweled comb. At last, Lottie and Lurline stepped back to admire their handiwork. Lurline gave a long whistle of appreciation. "Boy, howdy, are you ever beautiful!"

Lottie burst into tears. "My little girl is all grown up." She dug into her pocket for another tissue.

"Everybody decent?" All three women jumped at the masculine call from the door.

Abigail grinned. "Come on in, Daddy."

She thought she detected a bit of a swagger in his step as her father entered the room in his rented finery. "Lurline," he said, "The photographer wants to get a picture or two of you and Phillip before the ceremony."

Lurline took one final peek in the mirror before starting toward the door. "Shouldn't be too much of a hardship to spend a little time with your big brother—seeing as how he's the handsomest man I've ever laid eyes on." She winked at Abigail and disappeared out the door.

Lottie was right behind her. "I'd better check on things in the sanctuary one more time."

"That's fine, Mother. I thought I'd have a chat with my little girl." Samuel closed the distance between himself and his daughter and caught Abigail's smooth hands in his rough ones. "Now come, let your father have a look at you. Goodness, you're lovely." His eyes filled with tears. "My Abby girl, a woman grown."

Abigail threw herself into his arms. "Oh Daddy. I'm so happy. Happier than I ever dreamed possible."

He cupped her chin in his hand and studied her. "Are you sure? Can you truly find success hidden away here in Dust Bowl?"

"I'm sure," she answered earnestly. "I have all I'll ever need. A precious, loving husband and a wonderful family make a fine start." An impish grin turned up the corners of her mouth. "It's like a wise man once told me. 'You don't have to go far away to be a success. After all, it isn't what you do or how much you make or even who you marry that makes you a success. It's Whose you are.'"

≥a

"Hey Abby, honey! Look here. You've made the society pages again. Your buddy Suzanne wrote you up in her column."

"Really? What's it say?"

Careful to keep the paper above the swirling water, Jarred used his best television newscaster voice to read, "'Yesterday, in the surprise move of the season that has everyone talking, *Herald* reporter Abigail Bradley wed childhood sweetheart Jarred Worth, after having amiably ended her engagement to millionaire Edward Winters only weeks before.'"

Jarred lowered the paper to ask, "Give it to me straight. Does this make me sound like a penniless poacher or what?"

Abigail laughed and flicked water at him. "If you're going to be a celebrity, you have to develop a thick skin. What else does it say?"

"'The ceremony was performed in the bride's family church in Dust Bowl before a capacity gathering of friends and family. The church was tastefully decorated in a profusion of white flowers and greenery.'"

He lowered the paper again to say, "I don't remember any flowers."

Abigail rolled her eyes. "Good thing we took pictures."

"'Dressed with trademark simplicity, Abigail wore an elegant gown of white satin—'

"Now, *that* I remember." He snapped the paper up in front of his face to deflect the splash his wife aimed at him.

"'Following a charming reception in the church fellowship hall, the couple departed for their honeymoon to an undisclosed location.

"'Sources inside the *Herald* report Mrs. Abigail Worth named a successor for her weekly column before leaving. Lurline

Pettigrew, formerly of Obituaries, will fill Mrs. Worth's post as of January first.'

"Hey, honey, neat trick getting Lurline your old job."

"She'll be wonderful. She has a real flair for writing, I'm afraid it's been buried in Obituaries." Abigail's eyes widened in horror. "Did I just say that?"

Jarred chuckled. "I wonder how she and Suzanne will hit it off? They didn't look too chummy at the wedding. I half expected Lurline to haul off and hit her."

Abigail smiled. "They'll just have to learn to get along now. It seems they share common ancestry."

"You've got to be kidding! Lurline and Suzanne? No way. They're as different as night and day."

"I'm serious. I'm a firsthand witness to the fact they both recently joined the family of God."

Jarred leaned forward to drop a kiss on her forehead. "You're a pretty special woman, Abby."

She felt goose bumps raise on her arms even though they were submerged in the warm, bubbly water. "Well, go on. Is that all it says?"

"Nope, one more paragraph. 'It's been a pleasure chronicling Abigail's time in the spotlight over the last few months. Her achievements socially and professionally are undeniable, and yet I believe it was only very recently that she found true success. We'll miss you, Abigail. God bless.'"

Abigail brushed a tear from her eye and declared, "Enough reading for today." She plucked the newspaper from his hands and threw it over the side. "After all," she said, grinning into his surprised face, "we're honeymooning."

Jarred pulled her into his arms. "Ah, paradise."

A Letter To Our Readers

Dear Reader:

In order that we might better contribute to your reading enjoyment, we would appreciate your taking a few minutes to respond to the following questions. When completed, please return to the following:

Rebecca Germany, Managing Editor
Heartsong Presents
P.O. Box 719
Uhrichsville, Ohio 44683

1. Did you enjoy reading *Something From Nothing?*
   - ❑ Very much. I would like to see more books by this author!
   - ❑ Moderately
     I would have enjoyed it more if _____
     _____

2. Are you a member of **Heartsong Presents**? ❑Yes ❑No
   If no, where did you purchase this book?_____
   _____

3. What influenced your decision to purchase this book? (Check those that apply.)

❑ Cover	❑ Back cover copy
❑ Title	❑ Friends
❑ Publicity	❑ Other_____

4. How would you rate, on a scale from 1 (poor) to 5 (superior), the cover design?_____

5. On a scale from 1 (poor) to 10 (superior), please rate the following elements.

___Heroine   ___Plot

___Hero   ___Inspirational theme

___Setting   ___Secondary characters

6. What settings would you like to see covered in **Heartsong Presents** books?_____

_____

_____

7. What are some inspirational themes you would like to see treated in future books?_____

_____

_____

8. Would you be interested in reading other **Heartsong Presents** titles?   ❏ Yes   ❏ No

9. Please check your age range:
   ❏ Under 18   ❏ 18-24   ❏ 25-34
   ❏ 35-45   ❏ 46-55   ❏ Over 55

10. How many hours per week do you read? _____

Name _____

Occupation _____

Address _____

City _____ State _____ Zip _____

Mistletoe, Candlelight, and True Love Await

Discover the joy of Christmas love with these collections of inspirational love stories—one historical and one contemporary—from eight cherished Christian authors. Trade Paper. Only **$4.97** each.

____ *An Old-Fashioned Christmas*
Historical Collection
Sally Laity—*For the Love of a Child*
Loree Lough—*Miracle on Kismet Hill*
Tracie Peterson—*God Jul*
Colleen L. Reece—*Christmas Flower*

____ *Christmas Dreams*
Contemporary Collection
Rebecca Germany—*Evergreen*
Mary Hawkins—*Search for the Star*
Veda Boyd Jones—*The Christmas Wreath*
Melanie Panagiotopoulos—*Christmas Baby*

HEARTSONG PRESENTS *TITLES AVAILABLE NOW:*

(If ordering from this page, please remember to include it with the order form.)